unloved

# UNLOVED
## THE UNLUCKY ONES

# MARLEY VALENTINE

# unloved

*usa today* bestselling author
## MARLEY VALENTINE

Cover design by PopKitty Design
Photographer: WANDER AGUIAR :: PHOTOGRAPHY
Model: Alex, Darien & Ken
Edited by Shauna Stevenson at Ink Machine Editing
Edited by ellie McLove at My Brother's Editor
Proofreading by Hawkeyes Proofing

This book contains mature content.

# DEDICATION

*To my readers, your support and excitement for my books never ceases to amaze me. I hope this one was worth the wait.*

*There is beauty in being bruised.*
*There is beauty in being brave.*
*There is beauty in being.*

— MARLEY VALENTINE

# AUTHOR'S NOTE

Like many of my books Unloved is a story about love and healing but also deals with some heavy topics. Please note that the following occurs off page:

- Suicide

Please note the following occurs on page:

- Grief and Loss
- Mentions of Suicide
- Addiction
- Recovery
- Relapse/Attempted Suicide

While each character in this book deals with their own personal issues, each of them deals with it within a safe environment, and a reliable support system. Even though the author has written these stories with as much accuracy as possible, please remember this is still a fictional piece of writing.

If you ever find yourself in a situation where you need help, please do not hesitate to reach out to your national help hotline.

If you need any extra information on the subject matter in this book, please email the author at marleyvalentine@marleyv-books.com

# PROLOGUE
## LENNOX

One Mississippi. Two Mississippi. Three Mississippi.

"Lennox, look at me," Frankie pleads. "I'm sorry."

*One Mississippi. Two Mississippi. Three Mississippi.*

I haven't needed to count myself down from a panic attack like this in years. It was an old habit, one I hadn't used in so long, because I'd gotten too comfortable and content; two things I knew better than to let happen.

Because people lie and people leave.

People *always* leave.

People always leave *me*.

Sitting on the edge of Frankie's bed, I keep my head down and my gaze averted. I can feel my eyes filling with tears. Tears I refuse to cry. Tears I *refuse* to let him see.

"I can't stay here," he says. "Arlo and I..."

His voice cracks at the mention of his boyfriend, and I feel a shameful amount of jealousy that Arlo has the power to make my brother leave and an overwhelming amount of sadness that I'm not enough to make him stay.

*One Mississippi. Two Mississippi. Three Mississippi.*

"I can't watch him ruin his life," Frankie says sadly. "I love him too much for that. And I need a fresh start, too, you know? I need to do something with my life." He gestures to me. "And you're going to be busy with college and football."

He's rambling at this stage, shifting between excuses and explanations he thinks I need to hear, but the truth is, none of them matter when the bottom line is still the same.

*He's leaving me.*

Large hands sit atop my knees as Frankie crouches down in front of me, forcing me to raise my head and meet his gaze. Till this day, it catches me off guard how much we look alike, with our hazel eyes and chocolate-brown hair. I have no memory of our parents, so I don't know which one of them we take after, but there's no denying, the sadness on his face is an exact replica of my own.

"Len." He's the only one who calls me Len, everybody else always opting for my full name. "Please talk to me."

"I used to think I made you up," I say, the words catching me off guard. "Because there was no way I had a brother and didn't live with him."

"You know that was out of my control. I tried—"

I wave him off. "I know that."

And I do. Our years apart in different foster homes, living with different families, having completely different experiences, weren't on him. Since we'd come into each other's lives, he has been the best older brother, loving and caring for me in all the ways family should.

But, for some reason, it doesn't seem to alleviate the consuming amount of hurt that has settled inside my chest since he told me he was leaving Los Angeles. He's the closest thing to a parent I've ever had, and it feels like my parent is leaving me when I need him most.

All of this made me feel like a scared and insecure eight-year-old boy waiting around to be reunited with his brother, scared he wouldn't love me, certain that, like every other person in my life, he would leave me too.

I hated being that boy.

Wanting this conversation over and done with, I place my hands over his and push him away before standing. Inhaling a lungful of air, I straighten my spine and clear my throat, saying what I know he needs to hear and hoping it absolves him of his guilt.

"I don't want you to go," I admit. "But I understand why you have to."

He surprises me by stepping closer to me and grabbing my face, forcing our eyes to meet. "Why aren't you angry with me?" he asks.

"What are you talking about?"

"Why aren't you angry with me?" he repeats, his voice almost annoyed. "I spent years begging you to trust me, promising you I would never leave you. Why aren't you angry with me?"

Confused and frustrated, I wrap my hands around his wrists and push them off me. I'm four years younger than him, but I have a height advantage and my football training gave me size.

"What do you want from me?" I ask angrily, stepping into his personal space. "You want to go? So go. You want my blessing? You have it," I shout. "I don't know what difference you think it's going to make. Whether I'm angry at you or not, it isn't going to make you stay."

I run a hand over my face, irritation and anger making my blood boil. "You want to hear that I want you to stay? You want to hear that I'm mad that you're leaving? No." I shake my head vehemently. "You don't get to hear those things from me if they don't end up making a difference."

I step away from him, needing the space, trying to calm myself.

"Does it make a difference?" I ask once more, steadying my voice. "If I ask, will you stay?"

The silence adds salt to my already open and exposed wound.

I hold his gaze, reading the shock and heartbreak in every line on his young face. There is no hiding how out of character my outburst is for the both of us. I always keep my cards close to my chest, constantly living in fear that any inconvenience I might cause would have me back in foster care and alone. Even at eighteen, aged out of the system, with a football scholarship, a roof over my head, and a job, I can't shake that irrational fear that one day it will all be taken away from me.

"Like, I said"—I glance around the room, eyeing his bedroom door before allowing myself to look back at him—"I don't want you to go, but I understand why you have to."

I don't allow myself to linger or give myself the chance to worry about whether or not his feelings are hurt, because mine are too. It's time to be selfish and protect myself.

The damage is done; he's leaving me.

Lowering my head, I step around him and head to the door.

"Len," he calls out.

I ignore him.

"Len," he repeats, my name filled with enough anguish, I pause, my hand on the doorknob. "I know it doesn't help, but I am truly sorry."

A lone tear I'd been desperately trying to hold on to, rolls down my cheek.

I'm sorry too, because he is the first person I opened up my heart to, and with the way I feel now, he'll be the last.

# 1

## SAMUEL
### FOUR YEARS LATER

I can't breathe.
*Lennox.*
I can't breathe.
*Lennox.*
I can't breathe.
Pulling at the neck of my jersey, I gasp for air. Lungful after lung-
ful, I try, but my chest continues to constrict. Tighter and tighter.
I can't breathe.
*Lennox.*
One second, the home crowd's cheering, all of us watching as
Lennox runs up the length of the field, ball in hand. And the next, the
USC cornerback runs at him, shouldering him in the chest, hard
enough their helmets clash together, causing Lennox's body to
become airborne, looking for somewhere to land.
It's a textbook play. He's supposed to land on his back and get
right back up, but the force of the hit seems to have caught him off
guard, and his head thumps on the ground first, followed by his
shoulder and then the rest of his body.

All of him lands in a hard heap, one that has all the medical stuff running to him.

I expect him to move. To scream. To shout. But there's nothing.

*One Mississippi. Two Mississippi. Three Mississippi.*

"Sam, buddy. Try and breathe, okay? You got this."

It's the first time my brain has registered anything other than the scene in front of me.

The voice returns.

"Try it," it soothes. "Breathe in and out."

As if my head has been underwater and finally broken through the surface, my senses slowly return to me.

"That's right. Just like that," someone instructs. "In and out."

My head turns to find Jennings, one of our teammates, right behind me. His body is firmly pressed against mine, his arms wrapped around my broad shoulders, his voice right in my ear.

"Now, one more time," he coaxes. "You've got this. In and out."

It's in this moment, as his words hit me with clarity, that I realize my chest is finally rising and falling. Breaths moving in and out, in perfect sync with his words.

I don't know how I found myself being held back by him, but my gaze darts back to where I was obviously trying to run to.

I need to get to him.

I need to see what's wrong.

I need to wake him up.

I need to *touch* him.

God, I'm desperate to touch him. I always have been. An image of him at halftime, tipping his head up to the sky as he downed a whole bottle of water before winking at me and running back onto the field, freezes in my mind.

I wanted my fingertips to follow the beads of sweat down his cheeks, and the pad of my thumb to collect the few drops of water that sat there, waiting for me, on his pillowy bottom lip.

I should've touched him.

Not just today, but *every* day.

I should've told him how I feel.

*I should've.*

*I should've.*

*I should've.*

Before I know it, my body attempts to leap forward, and Jennings's arms coil around me like a snake, but my limbs whip into a frenzy, trying to get to Lennox.

"Lennox!" His name roars out of me, the word finally clawing its way out of my windpipe. "Lennox!" I scream again, this time thrashing my whole body, determined to rid myself of Jennings

"Samuel, buddy, you got to hold still and wait for the team doctors to work their magic and get him off the field."

"Let me go," I cry out. "Get your fucking hands off me."

If everyone wasn't already staring at us, they are now. Now that I can breathe and the shock has subsided, my hysteria is uncontainable.

My head can't reason with the reality that injuries on the football field happen all the time. I can't reason with the fact that everybody running toward him knows what they're doing and how to fix him.

None of that rationale matters, because each second that passes feels like long, agonizing minutes, each one more painful than the one before.

"We get concussions all the time," Jennings says, attempting to reassure me. "Some smelling salts and he'll be up in no time."

If my brain was actually working, I could tell myself just how many times a season this happens. But there is a complete disconnect, fear overriding logic, my head telling me to try and take a breath, but my heart telling me that something is very, very wrong.

The hit was hard, and the fall was harder. And he *still* isn't moving.

"Get. Off. Me," I say through gritted teeth.

"No," he says, his voice firm like his hold on me. "The team doctors are with him, and if you calm down, you can see they're assessing the damage and trying to wake him up."

The thought of being with him, by his side, slows my breathing down almost instantly. Roughly, I shake Jennings off me, and surprisingly, he drops his hands and steps back, giving me the space I so desperately need.

My body moves, pushing through the people, my arms and legs racing to get to him.

"Lennox," I shout as I step closer to him, hoping my voice alone can be the thing that has him opening up his eyes.

My stomach roils at the sight of him. They keep his helmet on but remove the facemask, ensuring his airway is as free as possible. Even though his eyes are still closed, I don't miss the sight of blood dripping down the length of his face as the man kneeling beside him waves smelling salts underneath his nose.

"Come on. Come on. Come on," I mutter, my body trembling as I wait. "What's taking so long?"

"Son, move out of the way and let them do their job." Coach sidles up beside me, his hand curling around my bicep, moving me back, away from Lennox. "The quicker they get him to wake up, the quicker they can fix him."

*Fix him* my brain chants. *Fix him. Fix him. Fix him.*

His eyes begin to flutter, long, slow blinks, and before I even have the chance to decide to move forward, Jennings is back, arms around me, holding me still.

"Give them a second," he says, his voice hard and commanding. "You are of no use to them or him right now."

I can feel myself shaking within his hold, watching paramedics run onto the field, joining the team doctors and coaches. The juxtaposition of everybody moving at warp speed around me, but Lennox's reactions and response time getting slower and slower by the second, is the final nail in the coffin.

"Something's wrong with him," I hear myself say.

"Well, yeah, he just got a mad hit to the head," Jennings responds, much too flippant for my liking.

Not wanting to jostle him, they keep him as still as possible while bringing a light to both his eyes and checking his pupils.

I watch them move from left to right, hoping for it to provide me with some relief, but it only amps up my anxiety even more.

While his eyes are open and he's responsive, there's no disguising Lennox's fear.

"No," I insist. "It's something else. Something is wrong."

"Okay. On three," I hear one of the medical staff say as he and another man hold on to either side of Lennox's body to place him on the backboard.

"One, two, three," they shout in unison. They lay his body down firmly, and I wait for the commotion to bring forth any other reaction out of him, but there's nothing. No wince of pain, no cry for help, just fear.

"Jennings, man, I need to—" I try to catch my breath as I watch the staff take him off the field, knowing I can't be away from him for another second. "Jennings. I need to follow them. If he's going to the hospital, I need to go with him."

"We still have a game to play—"

Tearing my gaze away from Lennox's retreating body, I use all my strength to push Jennings off of me.

He stumbles back, managing to stop himself from falling.

"Okay," he concedes, putting his hands up in surrender. Whatever expression I'm wearing causes his eyes to soften, a mixture of pity and sympathy staring right back at me. He gestures to the tunnels. "Go. What you do is none of my business anyway."

On autopilot, I run across the field, down through the tunnels, past the dressing rooms, and follow the muffle of voices into the team's medical room.

"Excuse me, you can't—" One of the team doctors, Randy, recognizes me. "Samuel, this isn't the time."

"Please," I breathe out, exhaustion finding me quickly. I walk into the room, ignoring all eyes on me, and closer to Lennox. "He's my boyfriend."

The lie tumbles out of my mouth with such ease, the words full of wishful thinking.

Aware of our college's recent campaign to ensure LGBTQ+ students are welcome and comfortable on campus, especially in sports, I know even if the team doctors wanted to push back and kick me out of the room, they're hesitant to do so.

Not bothering to wait for a response, I slip Lennox's limp fingers between mine, focusing on the fact that his skin is warm, and feel for his thrumming pulse.

"Sam." His voice is panicked as I come into view, and the sound of it has my heart falling to my stomach in relief, my body shaking with adrenaline.

I glance down at him, his eyes, still filled with fear, staring back at me. "I'm here. Everything's going to be okay."

His eyes widen at my words and his hand tightens in mine, forcing the moment of relief I felt only seconds ago to disappear. I store the fact that he can squeeze my hand to the back of my mind.

"Something's wrong, isn't it," I state, dragging my eyes up and down his body. "Is it your legs? Can you feel them?"

His mouth opens, but nothing comes out. Instead, his body begins to tremble, almost like his bones are rattling inside his skin. Lennox's chest rises and falls rapidly as he struggles to catch his breath.

"What's wrong with him?" I say a little too loudly in the small room. "He can't breathe. Why can't he breathe?"

Irritated, the team medic pushes me out of the way, dislodging my hand from Lennox's. "I'm sorry, Samuel, but if you want to be here, you need to sit on the other side of the room and keep out of the way." Another staff member comes back into the room, one of them now at either side of Lennox's body.

"If Lennox is having trouble breathing," he continues, "we need to get that under control and take his helmet and shirt off safely in case he has any other injuries."

"He squeezed my hand," I blurt out. "He can move his hands," I shout as I reluctantly move into the background, my view of Lennox becoming limited as I stare at the backs of all the doctors.

"Lennox. Lennox, can you look at me? Look at me and try to breathe," Randy instructs.

"Sam," he gasps loudly. "Where's Sam? I need Sam."

"I'm here," I call out as Randy says, "He's right here, Lennox, but I'm going to need you to try and keep still."

I watch him flail against the backboard, proof he isn't paralyzed, which should be a relief, but everything still seems extremely risky. Randy tries to keep him still and calm him down, but he doesn't stop asking for me. Over and over, his voice getting louder and louder, almost like he can't...

"He can't hear," I say.

The realization slips out of my lips quietly enough that it could've been mistaken for an internal thought. Randy and the other medic continue to try and calm Lennox down, and I know for certain now nobody has heard me.

"He can't hear," I say again, louder. "Stop talking to him," I shout. "He can't hear."

Not caring about protocol, or anything else but Lennox, I stride to them, ensuring I'm in Lennox's line of sight as soon as possible.

Lennox and I reach for each other's hands at the same time. He squeezes, and I just sit and wait, breathing in and out, making an exaggerated effort to show him the rise and fall of my shoulders.

We both ignore everything around us, and eventually, he figures it out and his desperate gasps for air regulate into a steady inhale and exhale. But almost like he's moved from one physical reaction to another, tears start to fall down the side of his face.

"Samuel," he says, his chin trembling, his voice full of fear. "Samuel."

Swallowing hard, I muster all my strength as my hands and fingers move of their own volition, wordlessly responding to him to show him I'm here—skating my fingers across his bloody eyebrow, wiping his tears, touching his lips, before resting my palm right above his beating heart.

*I'm here.*

He places his hand over mine, his water-filled eyes staring right at me. "Sammy."

There's been only one other time he called me Sammy, and it had caused my heart to dance and my blood to thrum. It was everything this moment wasn't.

"Sammy," he says again, his voice a little more steady. "I don't think..." He momentarily squeezes his eyes shut before looking at me again. "Sammy, I can't hear anything."

# 2

## LENNOX

I know the words leave my mouth, but it's jarring to realize that I can't hear myself say them. It makes me wonder if I whispered them and if anybody actually heard me.

"Sammy," I say in a rush. "Did you hear me? I can't hear."

He nods, and while the confirmation that he heard me and I didn't hear him shatters me on the inside, I do my very best to focus on his touch and his presence; the only things calming my racing heart.

My mind refocuses on the play against USC, the fall, and the aftermath, as I siphon through every moment, searching for any clue that can explain exactly how I ended up here. My hand remains clasped with Samuel's as the medical team slowly takes off my helmet, and then removes my shirt and shoulder pads. I know they'd be giving me updates every step of the way if I could hear them, but for now it's obvious they're banking on Samuel keeping me calm as they itemize my injuries.

When my helmet comes off, I catch sight of all their eyes widening.

"What is it?" I ask. "What's wrong?"

Without thinking, Samuel's mouth opens to tell me, but he catches himself at the last minute, brushing his fingers against my ear and then moving them in my line of sight so I can see.

"My ear's bleeding?"

He nods.

I'm surprised by the relief this news provides me. It's not an answer, but it's a start.

A hand grazes over my collarbone and I wince. On instinct my head tilts toward the pain, and I'm surprised to realize it hurts; quite a lot.

Randy says something to his assistant, and the man leaves and comes back with his phone. The screen shows his notes app and the words **We think your collarbone is broken** have been typed up on the screen.

The assistant returns to typing on the phone while Randy maneuvers my arm so my forearm is pressed against my chest.

I try my hardest to be patient, but frustration simmers below the surface, threatening to turn into anger; anger he doesn't deserve, but that I can't restrain.

With every passing minute, my life is changing before my very eyes, almost too fast to even adjust.

In tune with me like no other, Samuel releases my hand and takes the phone. He then looks at Randy and his assistant and points to the door. His mouth is moving, and even if I can't hear the exact words, his request is not lost on me.

They exchange words back and forth, the conversation clearly heated, but watching Samuel advocate for me fills me with a warmth I didn't think I could feel amongst all this rage. Eventually, they walk out of the room and Samuel sits on the edge of the examination bed.

I watch him talk into the phone and then he passes it to me.

My eyes scan the screen.

**They think your collarbone is broken and maybe you were so distracted by your hearing that your body didn't register the**

**pain. They're almost certain you're not hurt anywhere else, but they want to check you one more time before we go to the hospital. We need to do something about the break and to work out what's going on with your ears.**

I hand him back the phone, and with as much energy as I can muster, I turn on my good shoulder and push myself up. My body aches, but there's nothing alarming enough to keep me sitting here. Keeping my arm close to my chest, I swing my legs off to the side and hop down. I momentarily lose my balance, but Samuel is right there.

"I'm okay," I assure him.

He narrows his eyes at me and raises the phone to his mouth, speaking into it. I wait for him to turn the screen toward me, trying to not let my impatience show.

**They're not going to be happy with you walking around like this. At least see what Randy has to say before we leave. I need to get our bags from the locker room anyway.**

I don't want to stay, and I don't care about what Randy has to say, but I do want that look of worry and fear to disappear from Samuel's face.

I'm not used to him looking at me like that or treating me with kid gloves. He's my best friend, my equal, and there is no way in hell I'm letting whatever this is change that.

"I'm not lying back down," I say petulantly, as if it even matters.

He nods, then walks out the door. Only a few seconds pass before Randy comes back in, the cell phone now his new accessory.

He hands it to me.

**We're going to call the ambulance to pick you up so you don't have to wait too long in the emergency room. They'll strap up your arm properly and do enough tests to work out what's going on with your hearing and make sure you're not injured**

**anywhere else. I know Samuel is with you, but do you want us to call your family?**

*My family.*

It shouldn't have been a complicated question, but something about it is like kicking a hornet's nest. I'm twenty-two years old and I still refer to myself as a foster kid; the mention of family always taking me back to the past, remembering all that I lost in order to get to this point in my life.

My parents, my foster parents... Frankie.

When I was eight years old, I was reunited with my biological brother, Frankie, where we lived in a group home together along with Arlo, Clem, and Remy.

The connection between all five of us was unbreakable, or so I thought. Arlo and Frankie aged out of the system first and then Clem and I, followed by Remy. The plan was to all live together while each of us found our footing in the world, all of us being there to support one another.

And for the most part it all went according to plan.

Except Arlo and Frankie fell in love, broke each other's hearts, and Frankie moved to Seattle. Away from us. Away from *me*.

Objectively speaking, I always understood why he left, but as his younger brother, whom he moved heaven and hell to be reunited with, I will never understand why he didn't ever ask me to go with him.

It's been four years of pretty much radio silence between the two of us. No visits on the holidays, no weekly FaceTime calls, no daily texts. He'd tell you he's giving me space after knowing how much he hurt me by leaving, and I would say he just flat out abandoned me.

Potato, potahto.

Randy shoves the phone in my face again, bringing me back to the present, and I know he wants an answer to his question.

"Samuel will call my family," I tell him.

He nods just as Samuel returns to the room. Knowing he heard what I just said, I look at him pointedly. "Call Clem, please. But tell her not to call Frankie."

———

*Where am I?*

The thought disappears as quickly as it came, my heart beating wildly inside my chest, my lungs struggling to inflate. Unease settles over me as I try to calm myself down, remembering where I am and what I'm doing here.

*One Mississippi. Two Mississippi. Three Mississippi.*

My eyes frantically dart from object to object, the hospital room eventually taking shape around me. While my mobile hand reaches for my ear, tugging at the lobe, almost like the movement will change the outcome of the last however many hours I'd been here.

News flash: It doesn't.

Thankfully, my collarbone didn't need surgery and will heal on its own in a sling and with some regular icing, but it's truly the least of my worries. The longer I'm here, the longer I stew in my anger. Everything takes twice as long now that I can't hear, the stopping and the starting, sometimes even the slightest dismissal in my presence has me on a knife's edge. The initial shock has well and truly worn off, and reality is something I have no desire to face.

Shifting my body in frustration, I try to turn over, but pain courses through me, my shoulder and elbow throbbing in protest. I grunt as every bone and muscle aches, but instead of hearing the sound echo around the room, I feel the rumble at the back of my throat and the clench of my jaw, but I don't *hear* anything.

As the pain of my broken collarbone subsides, my eyes manage to land on the sleeping form in the corner of the room. With his arms crossed over his chest and his ankle resting on his knee, Samuel is two sizes too big for the chair he's currently squashed himself into.

The sight of him has me pressing pause on the constant stream of hurt and confusion that's been fogging up my brain since I arrived at the hospital and just taking him in.

No longer in his football gear, he wears gray sweatpants and a blue UCLA hoodie. I don't get to just stare at him often, and definitely not without him noticing. He is quintessentially good-looking —easy on the eyes with his blond hair, blue eyes, and a body that could only come from our grueling exercise regimen and strict lean diet. He is the All-American boy, with the bright eyes and carefree smile that he saves for me.

We've been best friends since our first day of college, and I think I was already in love with him on the second. It's stupid and going absolutely nowhere, but I can't shake it. I know he doesn't feel the same, because he told me exactly that, but my heart feels safer being caught up in his unrequited love than ever giving it to someone else.

He might not be in love with me, but he loves me in his own way, and the way he prioritized my well-being over absolutely everything else today will always be enough for me.

I watch as he stirs in his chair, his foot falling off his knee, his eyes rushing to open. In only a short amount of time, I've already noticed how much I've changed. My eyes work overtime taking everything in, not realizing how certain sounds could easily fill in the blanks.

I grab my phone off the overbed table and send him a message. Texting is a lifesaver, but it still doesn't fix the discomfort that comes when people talk around me or I'm the only person in a room speaking.

> You should go home and sleep in a proper bed.

He drags his cell out of his pocket, reading and typing back.

> Stop telling me what to do.

Smiling, I text back.

> I'm being serious. You can even sleep at my place instead of going back to the dorms.

Instead of texting back, Samuel drags his chair even closer and squeezes my thighs.

He shakes his head. It's a simple no that conveys everything.

*I'm not leaving you.*

He reaches for his phone again, and I feel my cell vibrate against the mattress.

> Why didn't you tell me about Frankie?

Shame washes over me for keeping a secret of this magnitude from Samuel. He knows almost everything about me, and it's not like I didn't want to tell him; it's more like I stupidly tried to forget Frankie exists.

When I met him, the abandonment was fresh, and I was jaded and being childish. On purpose, I stopped talking about Frankie with Clem and Remy, and it was even easier with Arlo because he was busy trying to push down the hurt Frankie caused him too.

Eventually, Frankie was off-limits and thoughts of him faded into the background.

"I'm sorry," I say, even if I can't hear the sincerity in my own voice, I hope he can hear it. "He's my brother. My *biological* brother," I emphasize, and this additional piece of information has Samuel straightening.

"He and Arlo were together," I continue. "But something went down between them and he decided to move to Seattle.

"I was eighteen when he left, and I haven't really ever gotten over him leaving me."

The words are the most honest thing I've said about the whole situation. Ever.

If I let myself think about it too much, I'm embarrassed by how much Frankie's departure bothers me. It makes me feel petulant and weak, and despite how hard I pretend to be unbothered by it, every-body, including Samuel now, knows the truth.

Samuel squeezes my thigh again and then sends me another text.

I raise the phone to my face, and my shoulders slump at the words on the screen.

> I'm sorry, but Clem called him.

I knew she would. Clem has been waiting in the wings, since the moment he left, for any reason to force his hand to come home.

Swallowing hard, I try to talk past the thick ball of emotion stuck in the back of my throat.

"I'm not ready, Sammy."

Without missing a beat, another text comes through.

> Then I'll make him wait till you are.

# 3
## LENNOX

Frankie is here.

I told you not to call him.

I'm not turning him away after he's come all this way.

All this way? Seattle is hardly "all this way."

Lennox...

Clem...

C lem hasn't let up since arriving at the hospital. Truth be told, she's being an insufferable mother hen, and I constantly have to remind myself it comes from a good place. She's worried about me, and I can't blame her because I'm worried about me.

But her insistence on making this the reason Frankie comes back from Seattle isn't something I want any part of.

I don't want to see him. I don't want to run the risk of needing my brother. I want to hold on to my anger toward him, because that is the only thing I want to feel. I'm teetering on the edge, my emotions alternating between anger and fear of the unknown.

I throw my cell on the bed, completely fed up with the back and forth of texting. "Can you please tell her to come in?"

Samuel raises an eyebrow at me, and I gesture to the door in frustration. "Clem. Please."

Completely unfazed by my attitude, he nods and wordlessly rises up from his seat and walks out of the room.

Guilt surges through me as I think of how many times impatience and frustration have consumed me, and how many times I've taken it out on Samuel, even though he's done nothing to deserve it.

Reaching for my phone, I quickly type a message out to Samuel, knowing he'll see it at some point.

> I'm sorry for snapping.

The door opens, and Clem walks in, Samuel and Remy both on their phones, trailing in behind her. My cell beeps, and I swipe at the screen, reading Samuel's response.

> You can make it up to me later. ;)

I feel my mouth stretch into a shy smile. Something about the way Samuel's text comes across like he's awkwardly flirting with me, changes my mood immediately.

I try to hold on to the warm feeling as I type back a quick text to him and then focus on Clem.

> You can count on it.

My smile doesn't go unnoticed, and when I glance up at Clem, she's smirking at me, knowing full well who I've got hearts in my eyes for. My infatuation for Samuel isn't a secret, not even from him, but his rejection is. I haven't told a single soul about how we would never be, choosing to live in this fantasy land where his friendship will forever be enough. Because even if things between us are complex, and we're still as close as ever, the reality that I opened myself up to another person—after I swore I never would again— and was turned away, makes my abandonment issues the very front and center of my life.

Pushing aside all those complicated thoughts and feelings, I reach for the tissue box and throw it at her, and just like that, the tension between us is broken.

Because that's how we are. She pushes, and we all eventually surrender. I have no doubt that's exactly how she managed to get Frankie here.

"He can come up and see me," I tell her. "But don't expect any miracles, okay? I have nothing to say to him."

My phone vibrates in my hand, and I look down to see a text from Samuel.

> I won't leave you alone with him unless you want me to.

I want to respond with a million heart emojis because that's what his care for me makes me feel. Instead, I opt for a simple "thank you," hoping those two words truly convey the gratitude I feel.

Clem's response to my conditions pops up on my screen.

> I'll take it. Thank you.

We offer each other sad smiles, the only true expression to the way I know we both feel inside.

Nobody loves like Clem loves. Her loyalty has no bounds, and even though we often fight exactly like siblings do, she's also the closest thing I've ever had to a mother.

When she arrived at the hospital to meet us after I got hurt, the heartbreak was written all over her face. Her worry and sadness over me, made me feel guilty for being injured. I knew what happened was an accident, but Clem didn't deserve to be sad or worried or anxious, especially over me.

Catching my gaze, Clem tilts her head to the door, signaling she's going to go and get Frankie. That leaves me with both Remy and Samuel in the room, and as much as I love everyone's round-the-clock support, the need to constantly be attached to my phone to ensure I don't miss anything is weighing on me.

It's been twenty-four hours of nothing but doctors and nurses running test after test and me waiting for results. I sat through both a CT and MRI scan to confirm my collarbone break and to determine no other bones or muscles of mine were injured from the tackle, but still no word on my hearing.

Neither the hospital staff, the coaching staff, or Samuel were impressed by my decision to "recklessly" get up and walk without being properly examined. I'd like to say they've been working tirelessly, but this isn't some medical television drama where a plethora of doctors are assigned to me and the wait times are almost non-existent.

No, this is real life, proving once again, it loves kicking you when you're down.

Feeling defeated, I sink into the pillows propped up behind my back, taking in my surroundings, trying so hard to just let myself breathe.

*One Mississippi. Two Mississippi. Three Mississippi.*

My collarbone throbs, but short of keeping it in this sling and taking painkillers, there's nothing I can do about it. I'm overwhelmingly tired, my mind and body on the verge of complete exhaustion, but I'm too scared to sleep.

The quiet is too much. I can't hear anything, my anxiety is on high alert, and my mind cannot accept the fact that I can't hear those small little squeaks and creaks that urge you to wake up when something is going on around you.

I don't want to think about this being permanent. I don't want to think that thought into existence, but doing that requires even a sliver of hope. And that is something I don't have.

The hospital door slowly opens, and my heart begins to beat wildly. My gaze darts to Samuel, who's staring right at me. Without a single word leaving my mouth, he rises up off his chair and comes to sit on the edge of the bed. His back is to the door and all his attention is on me.

He's the strength I need.

My gaze shifts back to the door, and I watch as Frankie walks in behind Clem, every step of his filled with trepidation. My traitorous chin quivers at the sight of him. *Fuck, how I've missed him.*

He's aged some, his sense of style a little more formal than I'm used to. He's grown into a man, one who has clearly spent time searching for and finding himself.

He raises his hand awkwardly, and it takes a great deal of effort to remind myself I'm mad at him. Forcing myself to lean into my petty feelings, I choose not to wave back. He might be here to help and do damage control, but I have no desire to make it easy on him.

Firm in my decision, I wait him out.

Clem is the first one to break, widening her eyes at me expectantly.

I don't give an inch.

When my silence becomes too much, I watch him step around Clem and drag his cell out of his pocket.

I anticipate the vibration but choose to open the message at my own slow pace. I pretend not to notice that our last message exchange was almost twelve months ago. What I don't do is tamp down the onslaught of rage that burns through me at the sight of his message.

I'm so sorry.

My hand moves of its own volition as I pick up my phone with my good arm and launch it at him. Despite the utter shock on his face, he manages to catch it, his mouth wide open, staring at me.

I don't want his stupid apology. I don't want his pity visit. There isn't a single thing I want from him, except for him to stay gone. Because if Frankie is gone, then it means there's nothing wrong.

But Frankie's here, with his stupid apology and pity visit. Frankie's here... and everything is wrong.

# 4
## RHYS

"How are you feeling today?"

As a twenty-seven-year-old addict, I've already been through a handful of sponsors. I stare at my newest sponsor, her black braids falling over her shoulder, making her look too young to make this work.

She would be one of many, because they never stick and I never stay sober.

I want to. Well, I think I do, but somehow I always end up right back here, someone asking me how I'm feeling and me feeling all too much.

I want to spill my guts, I want to lay it all out on the table for her, but the shame consumes me. I'm a spoiled brat, who got hooked on pain pills because I wanted to take them for fun.

I wasn't even in pain.

But now, pain is all I feel.

I want to crawl out of my skin. I want to set myself on fire. I want to run. I want to hide. I want to live, yet some days I want to die. But I can't say any of that. I lost that right. I lost the right to complain about all the ways drugs had ruined and controlled my life, when every moment leading up to this point has been a choice.

The wrong choice.

But a choice nonetheless.

One I took. And one I regret.

Well, I think I regret it, but clearly not enough to stop, right?

"Rhys." Jenika's voice cuts through my thoughts and I drag my gaze up to finally look at her. "Are you okay?"

A humorless chuckle slips from my mouth. "You've asked two of the hardest questions in less than five minutes."

"What would you rather I ask?"

"Nothing," I answer bitterly.

"Okay. Silence it is." She reaches into her bag and pulls out what appears to be a laptop. "I've got some work to do."

Jenika opens the laptop and sets it on the table in front of her. She sips on her coffee as she waits for whatever it is on the screen to load. Her hands start gliding across the keyboard, and for the next ten minutes she doesn't even give me a second glance.

It's what I want, isn't it?

My knee starts bouncing, and out of habit I start to bite at my cuticles. It's a disgusting habit. From the corner of my eye, I catch Jenika glancing at me, alternating between me and her computer screen.

When I've bitten my nails to the point of pain, I start frantically tapping a beat on the wooden table.

"Are you sure there isn't anything you want to talk about?" she asks.

"What's your story?" I blurt out.

It's not unusual for a sponsor and sponsee to discuss their journey to recovery, but Jenika is the only sponsor I've had that hadn't started out our introductions with her addiction story. It's where we're supposed to find common ground and feel seen, but all it does is make me feel stupid.

My mind is a minefield, and I know Jenika can see right through me. It makes shame course through me, but I try to push it away. I need her help to shift my mindset from that of an addict to that of someone in recovery.

I've been sober for three months, and I want—no, *need*—it to stay that way. Because the truth is, I don't think I can mentally survive another relapse.

My worry is that I don't know if I would want to survive.

Eyeing me, Jenika closes her laptop and pushes it to the side of our table. "My parents were addicts," she starts. "I started drinking and using at thirteen. I thought if I couldn't beat them"—she shrugs —"then I'd join them."

She reaches for her coffee and takes a quick sip before continuing. "We didn't have much, and I had access to more drugs and alcohol than I did food.

"You can see where this is going," she says. "Before I knew it, my whole life revolved around feeding my addiction. I was nothing but skin and bones."

"What changed?" I ask her, my question serving as a lifeline. Anything that could make me feel like I had hope and this would be worth it.

"I needed a new liver," she says matter-of-factly. "I unknowingly caught hepatitis B and C and ended up with liver cirrhosis."

She delivers her story with no emotion, something I'm not used to but find that I prefer. I realize I don't want the sugar-coated version or the watered-down one. I want cold hard truths and realities that are too close for comfort.

I *need* to know that everybody has an ugly side, because the happy ever after feels so fucking out of reach, I can't relate.

But being on death's door... I can relate to that.

"Did you get a new liver?" I ask.

"I wouldn't be here if I didn't."

"Are you happy?" My question takes me by surprise.

Jenika shifts on her seat, a sad smile on her face as she places her forearms on the table and leans forward. "What do you want to hear?"

"The truth."

"The truth is, there is no magic fix," she says. "And the definition of happy is different for everyone. Do I believe being sober will make you happier? Controversial take? No, I don't. But do I believe that your addiction is robbing you of all the ways you *could* be happy? Absolutely."

I ruminate on her explanation, thinking of all the things I've lost because of my addiction, understanding exactly what she means when she says addiction robs you of your happiness, or at the very least it robs you of the ability to even try.

"I kind of just tell myself if I wanted to be sober, I could be," I admit. "And if I keep failing, then I don't want it badly enough."

"I'm going to go out on a limb here and assume that you've been around a lot of people who have drilled this way of thinking into you time and time again," she says.

I think of my dad yelling at me over and over again, telling me just to man up and take responsibility for my life, not understanding that I truly would if I could.

"But what people forget to understand is that addiction is a disease." I don't know why, but my eyes fill with tears as I listen to her. "It's a sickness, and just like any other sickness, it needs to be treated. Getting help when you're sick isn't a weakness, Rhys."

Averting my gaze from hers, I clear my throat, trying to rid myself of the sudden onslaught of emotions overwhelming me. None of what she's saying is new. This is what going to rehab is all about. You detox, and you work through the root of your problems and talk about ways to confront them. You give yourself grace and find ways that inspire you to succeed.

Within the four walls of the rehab facility, and under the guidance and encouragement of all the staff, nothing feels impossible. And yet, every time I come face-to-face with the real world, I buckle.

"Tell me I can do this," I say, looking back at her, the vulnerability in my voice unmissable, but I'm sick of trying to pretend I have it together.

"Rhys." A look of determination settles on her face. "You can absolutely do this."

———

"Arlo." With my hands in my pockets, I call out to the man I've pseudo stalked the last few times I've visited the gym.

I couldn't tell you the last time I'd been in a gym or invested any time in caring about being healthy or what I look like. But after my initial meeting with Jenika, she suggested stopping by *this* particular gym and meeting with a guy named Arlo.

At the sound of my voice, he turns to look at me, narrowing his eyes, assessing who this stranger is walking up to him and who knows him by name. With a towel over his shoulder, he looks exactly like the type of guy you would expect to see at a gym: tall, broad shoulders, thick thighs, muscles for days.

"Hey, Arlo," I repeat as I get closer, extending my hand out for him to shake. It's my boldest move yet, introducing myself to a stranger and anticipating rejection.

"I've been checking out your classes," I tell him. "My friend Jenika recommended them to me."

His suspicion seems to disappear the second I mention Jenika, and it makes me wonder how much about her he knows.

"Is Jenika your sponsor?" he asks.

*Okay, well, that answers that question.*

Caught off guard, I drop my hand from his and dip my chin to my chest, trying to hide the embarrassment I can feel rising in my cheeks.

"Hey, man," he says gently. "We've all been there."

I know he's trying to make me feel better, and in a perfect world, his solidarity would, but the shame and disgust I so often walk around with, makes it almost impossible to be on the receiving end of any empathy.

"What is it that Jenika suggested?" he asks, trying to coax a conversation out of me. "If I know her as well as I think I do, she sent you here to fill up your free time."

This is true. It's harder to relapse if your mind is busy and your free time is occupied. I raise my head, my eyes meeting his. "She mentioned you could show me all the programs the gym has and I could decide on what would work for me."

He nods. "Usually, I would arrange a time that we could sit and talk, but I'm free now, if you are?"

"Yes, please." The words rush out as I nod vehemently, worried that if I don't do it now, I'll lose my nerve. "I'd love to leave here with a plan."

"Perfect." He tilts his head in the direction of what I assume is his office, and I dutifully follow. "Sorry I didn't get to ask before, but what's your name?"

Standing behind him, I watch as he searches for his keys in his pockets and unlocks the office door.

"It's Rhys."

Arlo pushes the door open, and I follow him inside. He gestures for me to take a seat on the small sofa located opposite the door.

Nervously, I take a seat and watch as he quickly sifts through a bunch of papers and slips them into a clipboard. He takes a seat in his office chair and wheels himself till he's parked in front of me.

"I've been meaning to streamline all this to have the intake forms be digital, but I keep procrastinating. Until then, this is for you." He hands me the clipboard and a pen. "These are so you can get your gym membership as soon as possible and the rest are questionnaires that will help you decide what goals you want to achieve while you're here."

I perch the clipboard on my thigh, not even noticing how much my leg is bouncing, and flick through the pages. The information requested isn't extensive or invasive, but my sobriety always brings about indecisiveness. I struggle with what I like and what I don't. I often feel like I don't really know myself, and I second guess everything, worrying I'm hindering progress without even realizing it.

Arlo waits patiently as I scan through the questions. There are some about my diet, asking if I want help with a nutritionist, and then there's one asking if I have a job.

I don't.

Every question feels like an indirect way of asking me if I'm taking care of myself and how I want to continue taking care of myself. I don't know either answer. I tick the boxes that make the most sense, and hope it's enough.

Improve my relationship with food? Check.

Focus on mental health? Check.

Want to make my body and mind a priority? Check. Check. *Fucking check.*

"How are these classes any different from what other gyms offer?" I ask.

"They're not," he deadpans. "The difference is in the people who attend and teach the classes. We're all in recovery."

"Everyone?" I ask skeptically.

I don't know why this shocks me, but it does. I've never been around others in recovery. I always end up relapsing before I have the chance to make any lasting connections with other people I can relate to.

"Everyone," he repeats. "If you need somewhere to go to help stop yourself from relapsing, this is the place for you."

"Why...?" Groaning, I run a hand over my face to stop myself from finishing the question.

"Why what?" Arlo asks.

"Why is everything so hard?" I sigh, absolutely defeated, losing my bravado and worrying if I can even manage something as simple as coming to the gym. "I wish getting high wasn't so much easier than getting clean."

He chuckles, and it's filled with complete understanding. He reaches for the clipboard. "Finished?"

Nodding, I hand it to him and fall back on the couch, tilting my head and looking at the ceiling.

*One Mississippi. Two Mississippi. Three Mississippi.*

I stew in my silence, and Arlo lets me, completely unfazed by the stranger in his office who's trying to find the meaning of life.

I want to do this. I want to get it right. And for the first time, in this room, I think maybe I can.

Shifting on the couch, I sit up, and Arlo, who is now sitting at his desk, looks up at me.

"Jenika speaks really highly of you," I say, interrupting the quiet. "Says you've really made a life for yourself."

Arlo's size is intimidating, but the small smile he manages and the slight blush of his cheeks are proof that we're all the same. I can tell it makes him uncomfortable, and truth be told, I understand why. For some of us, the self-hate and disappointment of how badly we fucked up our lives, overrides any achievements.

But that doesn't take away from the fact that I've now met two people who are successful and sober. It has a flicker of hope forming in my chest. I so desperately want to do this.

Stirring me out of my thoughts, Arlo rises up off his chair and walks around his desk. He gestures to the docr. "Let me show you around the place and then we can put together a plan that suits your schedule before you leave."

As he leads the way, I follow his every step and hang off his every word. I push down the inconvenient thoughts that tell me I can't commit; the very same ones that remind me I'm a failure.

Addiction is a disease.

I'm treating it.

*One Mississippi. Two Mississippi. Three Mississippi.*

I can do this.

I *will* fucking do this.

# 5
## SAMUEL

The doctor, Dr. Keriakos, couldn't have picked a worse time to come and discuss Lennox's prognosis. Lennox has yet to speak to me, but the way he lashed out at Frankie, has me on high alert. He's frustrated and hurt, and I can't differentiate if it's because of the last forty-eight hours or Frankie's return.

Right now, anger is rolling off him in waves, and whatever news the doctor has to give him, my gut is telling me it isn't going to be good. We've already been here too long, and the unanswered questions are piling up.

Pulling up a seat beside Lennox, the doctor places a manilla folder on the tray table and pushes it toward him. Lennox opens it at the same time the doctor drops a handful of pamphlets in front of him.

I send Lennox a quick text.

Do you want me to leave?

I see my message appear on his cell as it vibrates on the table between us. He glances up at me and shakes his head, then looks back at the endless amount of information the doctor has just given him.

"There's a lot of information here," the doctor says, surprising me when I realize he's talking and he's talking to me. "I'm going to leave all this information for Mr. York to digest, and when he's ready, we can start working through any questions he has."

I'm just about to tell the doctor off for addressing me instead of Lennox; his dismissal is extremely unprofessional. Before I get the chance to, a figure in the doorway catches my attention.

Frankie, like a dog with a bone, is back and just standing there expectantly. I turn to see Lennox's reaction, and he's looking at me, the request for help written all over his face. Standing, I stalk toward Frankie, who straightens his spine, pushing back his shoulders, determined to show me he won't back down.

He's on the defensive, ready to pounce, and if this wasn't a pivotal moment in Lennox's life, I would laugh at how ridiculous his older brother is being. I don't know what he thinks I'm going to do, but I have no intention of throwing down in Lennox's hospital room.

His mouth runs a mile a minute the second I reach him. "If you're going to try to tell me to get out, you better rethink your game plan," he says sternly. He points at Lennox, and I follow his stare to see anger and pain etched into every single one of my best friend's features.

Frankie gestures back to himself, pointing repeatedly at his chest. "He's my brother, and I'm not fucking going anywhere. Understood?"

Just like with the doctor, Frankie is not taking into consideration that his brother can't hear what he's saying. I don't like it, but unlike the doctor, I can see it's not intentional. His emotions are running high—everyone's are—and while I know there's history and so much hurt and regret between them, there's no missing how much Frankie loves Lennox.

Reminding us of his presence, Dr. Keriakos clears his throat, uncomfortable at the interruption. "Is everything all right here, gentlemen? Do I need to call security?"

Everyone's attention shifts to the doctor, including Frankie's, who extends his arm out and introduces himself.

"I'm Frankie York, Lennox's brother. I just arrived from Seattle and would appreciate being kept in the loop every step of the way."

Picking up on the tension, the doctor's gaze bounces between the brothers. "Since your brother is an adult, I will need his consent before passing along any of his medical information."

I watch Frankie swallow hard and slide his hands in his pockets, trying so hard to harness his feelings, knowing full well there is a high likelihood of Lennox withholding his consent.

"Do you think you both," he says, pointing at me and Frankie, "can give Lennox and me a few minutes alone?"

Reluctantly, I step outside, wondering if the good doctor will manage to succinctly work out how to effectively communicate with Lennox. The fact that he was so aloof when he first came in with all his pamphlets, doesn't leave me with much hope, but there isn't anything I can do.

Depending on the outcome, this is going to be a constant in Lennox's life—people assuming, people forgetting, people not really caring. It's a perspective I've never had a reason to acknowledge, and it makes me feel more than a little disappointed in myself.

But above all those things, I want to protect him. He's an adult; a boy who grew into the best type of man despite a continuous stream of hurdles he seemed to face. Finding out he has a brother he didn't mention to me had been a little bit of a blow to my ego.

But I would be a hypocrite to feel that way, knowing I'm keeping a secret from him too.

I push the guilt down, because this isn't the time or the place.

With Frankie and I now outside the hospital room, I expect it to be awkward, but Frankie surprises me when he turns to face me.

"Look," he starts. "I can see how protective you are of Lennox, and I appreciate it. More than you know."

I know we both have Lennox's best interest at heart, and whatever the reason is he and Lennox are estranged, not loving and caring for his brother isn't it. But if he thinks I'm just going to abandon Lennox, he's got another thing coming.

I interject. "If you're about to tell me you've got it handled from here on out and I can leave, I'm telling you now that isn't going to happen."

He doesn't seem to be too surprised by my outburst, but it does momentarily silence him.

"I can see you care about Lennox," he says, tone gentle. "And I'm grateful for that. Truly, I am. But I'm not trying to push you out. I'm just asking, albeit a bit forcefully, that he let me in."

Caught completely off guard by his reasoning and vulnerability, I feel the adrenaline of the last forty-eight hours rush out of me, and I lean on the wall behind me, using it for support. I slide my body down, crouching on the floor, and bury my face in my hands.

I'm scared and exhausted. And the truth of what Lennox is facing makes my chest ache for reasons that are so profoundly selfish, it fills me with shame.

None of this was supposed to happen. Not for us, and especially not for him. And not before I found the courage to tell him how I truly feel.

I am Samuel Hart, in love with his best friend, living in denial and so fucking full of regret.

I'd been scared and waited too long, and now he might never hear those three words from my mouth. I know telling Lennox now would come across as a knee-jerk reaction, almost pity-like, and he deserves better than that.

He deserved better all along.

I thought I could show up to one of the best universities in the country and pretend like the life I lived before that moment didn't matter. I told myself I was untouchable—Samuel Hart, son of Ramsey and Desiree Hart, living the American dream and attending UCLA on a football scholarship.

And then I met Lennox York.

I fell into Lennox on my first day of college, wide-eyed and excited. It wasn't love, but I was falling into something—I just didn't know it.

I didn't know I was capable of falling for a guy, and I didn't know I could fall so fast.

I'm so far from the untouchable person I thought I was. Sitting in this hospital, I'm closer to breakable than I've been in a really long time.

And I can't afford to be.

Frankie's voice interrupts my fall down the rabbit hole, and I turn my face to look at him.

"Why don't you go home for a bit?" he suggests. "Take a shower? Maybe even a nap? He knows you're here for him."

A war wages inside of me, exhaustion completely consuming me. I take in Frankie's face, so similar to Lennox's, with nothing but genuine understanding in his expression.

He places a hand on my forearm. "I promise I'm not going to shut you out. Just go home and give yourself a moment, and by the time you come back, Lennox and I will have it all worked out."

I run a hand down my face and sigh. "Fine," I concede, also wanting to give Lennox and Frankie the space to do and say what they want without an audience. "I'll go, but I'll be the one to tell him."

# 6

## LENNOX

My eyes stay trained on Frankie as he walks back into the hospital room sans Samuel, who's probably already home, showered and hopefully getting some sleep. I notice Frankie has also gone somewhere and freshened up, now wearing dark jeans and a gray tee, looking more comfortable than when he arrived. It makes me wonder where he's staying and for how long.

The tension in my shoulders tightens as he gets closer.

I'm not afraid of my brother, nor am I completely disappointed to see him, but I know the anger I'm holding on to is the one single reason keeping me from absorbing the severity of my situation and dissolving into a puddle of emotions I know I absolutely can't handle.

Dr. Keriakos thought the best way to inform me of my diagnosis was to hand me a manilla folder with everything written down. I appreciated the access to the information, and the ability to put a name to what was wrong with me, but I didn't realize how impersonal the exchange would make me feel.

He asked if I wanted Frankie to be kept in the loop, and the relief on his face when I conceded, had him out the door, talking to Frankie about me in no time.

Frankie awkwardly raises a hand in a shitty attempt of a wave, and if everything wasn't so tense between us, I would laugh at him. He quickly drops his hand, coming closer and sitting in the seat beside my bed.

On the tray table is a small whiteboard, the legal-sized pad of paper, and my cell, all my new methods of communication just waiting to be utilized. He surprises me when he picks up the white-board marker and writes on the mini board.

*Is this okay?*

"Do I have a choice?" I respond, certain that if I could hear my voice it would be full of snark.

He shakes his head and continues writing.

*We have to talk.*

*No shit, Sherlock. Is he seriously writing down everything on a white-board right now?*

"Text me," I say, reaching for my cell. "This is fucking ridiculous."

He plucks his own phone out of his pocket and begins to type whatever it is he wants to say. I watch him type and retype, and type and retype.

"If you're going to make such a fuss about talking to me, then just spit it out."

He chews on the corner of his lip, determination written all over his face. I wish I had a semblance of patience, but my insides feel like they're shaking with anxiety as I wait for him. His fingers move faster over the screen, and I hold my cell phone, almost crushing it between my fingers.

It's still vibrating when I eagerly look down at the screen, completely blindsided by his question.

> Before you got to the group home, did you get knocked around by your foster parents?

Squeezing my eyes shut, I feel nauseous almost immediately, my insides swirling like a whirlpool as I try to will the words on the screen away.

*One Mississippi. Two Mississippi. Three Mississippi.*

When I reopen my eyes, the words are still there and Frankie is still staring at me, waiting for an answer I'm unwilling to give.

Holding my gaze, his eyes are pools of pain, begging to understand. He sits on the edge of the bed now, placing a hand over mine, trying desperately to encourage me to have this conversation with him.

I pull my hand out from under his and turn my head to the side, avoiding him and avoiding the truth. As if he can't stand the thought of me struggling for a single second longer, he climbs up onto the bed, invading my personal space, waiting for me to turn my head back to face him.

*One Mississippi. Two Mississippi. Three Mississippi.*

Unshed tears fill my eyes, knowing I can't hide away from this much longer. I finally find the courage to look at him, and devastation mars his features. He stares at me, and I know the sight of me crying gives the answers I can't.

"I know I should've told you. But I..."

The words trail off into nothing, and Frankie wraps his arms around me, holding me as the memories I tried so hard to suppress resurface again.

The tears stream down my face freely now, turning into overdue sobs.

Secrets are no longer an option.

It doesn't matter that we're two grown men. It doesn't matter that we haven't spoken to each other in years. It doesn't matter that he, of everyone in my life, hurt me the most. Because right now he's my brother and the one person I need.

When we were reunited in the group home, I'd tried so hard to be the brother with no baggage, like everything before that moment to ever happen to me, never existed. Worried that if I was too much, Frankie would put me in the "too hard" basket. He was my saving grace. He was my one-way ticket out of hell.

*One Mississippi. Two Mississippi. Three Mississippi.*

"Why are you asking?"

Reluctantly, he pulls away and brings his phone between us.

> What I'm going to tell you might be a lot to take in, and I'm sorry. Tell me to stop when it gets too much and I WILL.

I read the words on his screen and nod.

> Dr. Keriakos said it was likely that the football injury contributed to your hearing loss, but it isn't the cause.

Confused, I try to connect the dots. "And what? Getting thrown around by my foster parents is?"

He winces at my admission, and I watch as he opens his mouth, but then quickly realizes his mistake, returning to typing furiously on his phone.

> You have a genetic degenerative condition. You would've lost your hearing eventually, no matter what, but getting knocked around, then and now, may have brought it on quicker.

"Do you have it?" I ask, selfishly wanting him to feel as shocked and off-kilter as I do.

He shrugs nonchalantly, like even if the answer is yes he

wouldn't care, and I hate that. I hate that he's so secure and so stable that nothing shakes him.

Despite the abundance of emotions I'm feeling, I continue to read the screen as Frankie continues to relay everything Dr. Keriakos told him.

> Your inner ear and nerves in your ears have been damaged over time because of the condition. Add in some decent blows to the head, and you now have what's called sensorineural hearing loss.

"The doctor told me what I have now, but he didn't say anything about a genetic condition. Why wouldn't he tell me that? Why didn't he ask me about my past?" I fire question after question, struggling to understand this new piece of vital information. "I'm the patient. Not you."

Frankie has the decency to look remorseful before answering my question.

> You told him he could talk to me.

The abuse was supposed to be the only secret. It was supposed to be left behind because it was a different life and a different Lennox.

"I thought he would be telling you stuff I already know," I spit out. "I'm sure this is a breach of confidentiality."

I know it isn't, but I'm feeling all types of things and clutching at straws to try and understand how I got here.

> What are you mad at? That I found out about the abuse or that it's genetic and you didn't know?

*What am I mad at?*

*What am I fucking mad at?*

"What am I mad at?" I roar. "Do you know what it's like to feel yourself boil over in anger and to know you're screaming and not be able to hear it? Do you know what it's like to wake up from a concussion and realize you can't hear a single fucking thing?

"And not only am I deaf, but it's also genetic and nobody knew because nobody gave a shit." I grab the Jell-O cup that's been sitting on the tray and throw it across the room, causing it to splatter against the wall. "Because once again, nobody gave a fuck about me."

I slump against the pillow in defeat and throw my arm over my eyes, my breathing shallow and labored.

"I can't do this, Frankie," I say, the words catching on a sob. "I can't fucking do this."

Frankie pulls me back into his arms, rocking us back and forth. I feel so helpless and small, like the child who was used as a punching bag, hoping that each passing day was the day things got better.

Tears uncontrollably stream down my face; I can't even stop them if I wanted to. The worst part is, I don't even know what I'm crying about. Is it the fact I lost my hearing, or is it everything I've endured that led to it?

As my crying subsides, I feel a shift in Frankie, and when I tilt my head up, I come face-to-face with a worried Samuel.

He glances down at me, and I offer him a sad but hopefully reassuring smile. I should be embarrassed, knowing my eyes are probably red and puffy, and there's no doubt I have snot running down my face. But if there was anyone other than Frankie who was ever going to know every single one of my truths, it's him.

Slowly, I peel myself off of Frankie, no longer caring that I'm a twenty-two-year-old man crying all over his brother's shoulder. I look between the two of them and feel so much dead weight lift off my shoulders.

"I need to sleep," I say, surprising them both. "Can one or both of you sit here with me while I do?"

They nod, and I know neither one of them is leaving my side. And I love them for it.

My eyes land on Frankie, and all the animosity between us disappears, as if the time and distance between us never happened.

Swallowing hard, he holds his hand out to me and I take it. We silently share thoughts as he squeezes my fingers tight, acknowledgment and understanding between us.

*Your secrets are safe with me.*

# 7
## RHYS

"Great job, man." Arlo slows down the speed on his treadmill, just as my machine stops beside him. "How do you feel?"

I rub my gym towel over my flushed face, trying to catch my breath. "I think I might die."

He chuckles. "It definitely feels like that in the beginning, but I promise you it will get easier."

Feeling like death, I down a whole bottle of water before responding. "I hope so, because I need a little bit of easy."

There's something about Arlo that has me running my mouth and saying things I immediately want to take back.

"Is everything okay?" he asks. We both step down off the treadmills and walk across the gym floor toward the lockers. "Are you attending regular meetings and talking to Jenika?"

I'm not used to anyone caring, or at the very least even prying, but if I let myself take Arlo and his questions at face value, it feels different. Not good, not bad, just different and a little less lonely.

"I am," I answer hesitantly.

"But..." he probes.

I shake my head. "Nothing."

"Are you doing this alone?"

Unlocking my locker, I hide my face inside while I try to avoid answering his question. "What do you mean by alone?"

"Like, do you have a support system? Friends? Family?"

My knuckles whiten as I grip the metal locker door. I don't care if it's obvious that I'm alone and have nobody supporting me, I'm not going to admit that to a stranger. I don't need to draw attention to all my flaws and all the reasons my family and friends walked away. I know enough about myself to know that giving Arlo the highlight reel of my past will not be conducive to my sobriety.

"Rhys," he says softly, and I flinch, needing to find a way to stop experiencing every single emotion at every single moment. I keep my head buried in the locker.

"Rhys," he repeats. "You don't have to answer my question. It was invasive and really none of my business. I'm sorry."

*One Mississippi. Two Mississippi. Three Mississippi.*

Eventually, I drag myself out of hiding, certain my anguish is written all over my face for Arlo to see. "I'm just not used to someone taking the time to ask if I'm okay," I admit. "It's all a lot to deal with right now."

"It is," he assures me, his voice filled with nothing but sincerity and understanding. "It might seem like nobody cares right now, but please remember that we might not be the people you thought would have your back, but we're here for you. In any way you need us to be."

I try to swallow down the ball of emotion in my throat as I nod, appreciating every single second of time people like Arlo and Jenika give me.

"Do you have my cell number?" he asks. My slow response time forces him to hold his hand out to me. "Here, pass me your cell, and if you need anything, anything at all," he reiterates, "even if it's an extra workout, just call me."

Handing him the phone, I stick my head back inside the locker, needing to avoid his attention. It doesn't matter if it's good or bad, I don't know what to do with it.

When the silence stretches for too long, I rear my head back and find Arlo's gaze. Looking at me pointedly, he lobs the cell phone at me and I catch it. "Call me."

It's not a demand, but the tone in his voice says it might as well be. I nod, once again feeling both grateful for the support and ashamed I need it in the first place.

Trying my damndest to not get caught up, stewing and over-thinking about every little interaction I have with someone, I nod at him, telling myself that his offer is genuine and if I need anything he'll be there for me.

Every day, I'm determined to face the day with so much energy and positivity, but by the time I put my head down on the pillow for the night, I'm nothing but an anxious mess, desperate to sleep and hide from the world.

The whole cycle is on rinse and repeat, and as the days progress, my lack of sleep has impacted my mood, and I've become a diluted version of the man I want to be. I'm trying to keep my head above water, but some days it feels like I'll forever be treading, trying to catch my breath and hold on, and failing.

Arlo's voice interrupts my wayward thinking. "Do you want to grab a bite to eat?"

As if he read my mind and threw me a buoy when I needed it most, I grab his offer with both hands and a smile.

"I have a few things I need to finish up here, but I could meet you somewhere in an hour or so," he says

"I don't mind waiting here," I tell him, worried that if I walk out of here, so will my resolve. "I can shower and wait."

"Okay," he nods. "Sounds like a plan."

He leaves and I sit down on a nearby bench with my phone in hand before showering. Staring at my screen, I open every single social media app I have and mindlessly scroll through, feeling completely removed from the posing and the smiles and just the sheer joy that's in every photo.

I know well enough it's all a front, and for every photo where someone is smiling and living their very best lives, there is a version of them that is imperfect and sometimes struggling. I know that, but I still crave the normalcy of it all. I don't want to stand out or be different; I want to blend in with the crowd any way I can.

Standing, I toss my cell into the locker with my bag, then grab a towel. Not wanting to make Arlo wait for me, I rush to the shower, washing my body and hair in record time.

I pick out the chinos and shirt I was wearing before I changed into my gym wear and hope they don't look too creased to sport in public, now that they've been folded in my bag.

With a quick glance in the mirror, I flick my wet hair every which way, when an errant thought has me in a state of panic. I've been out of the dating game for a while—actually, dating is probably the most inaccurate term of any of my interactions with people I'm interested in—but Arlo didn't ask me out on a date, did he? There would at least need to be interest from both parties or even an inkling of chemistry, right?

I'm not interested in Arlo, and I'm certain his friendship and niceties aren't him being interested in me beyond our shared experiences.

I don't think I would've gotten that wrong.

Giving up on my hair, I just run my fingers through it, ensuring the strands are brushed back enough so they're off my face. I look at my reflection one last time, and I don't miss the color in my cheeks and the small light in my eyes.

*I can do this.*

When I reach Arlo, I figure transparency is the best option, because whether I want to admit it or not, I need his friendship, and I don't want a stupid misunderstanding to jeopardize that.

"This isn't a date is it?" I blurt out.

Rendering him speechless, his mouth opens and closes, like a fish out of water.

"I mean, you're great and extremely attractive," I tell him. "But I—"

He raises a hand to interrupt me. "This isn't a date."

My shoulders relax almost immediately, and my relief makes Arlo laugh.

"Should I be offended by how relieved you are right now?"

"No. Shit. I'm sorry," I say, worried underneath the bravado that I've really upset him.

"I'm kidding," he assures me, a small smile on his face. "I know how it is when you're first trying to get your life together. And for the record, I don't do dating, or relationships, or really any kind of thing that distracts me from sobriety."

I don't know why this feels like a punch in the gut. Relationships are so far from my mind, but the idea of meeting someone, who makes you feel good, and having to push that away, makes me hate this journey just that little bit more.

"You think being with someone will ruin my sobriety?" I ask, the deflation in my voice impossible to hide.

"No." He grabs my shoulder and holds my gaze. "I think if *I* was with someone, it might ruin *my* sobriety."

I don't wholeheartedly believe he meant it only to apply to him, but I do my best not to let it bother me. I know there are a list of dos and don'ts and things that are encouraged and things that aren't. But for now, there's no point preempting a problem that I've yet to encounter. But as I push away these thoughts, I'm met with another.

I narrow my eyes at Arlo. "You really haven't been with anyone since becoming sober? How long's it been now?"

Without interrupting the conversation, Arlo walks us to the gym exit and talks at the same time.

"It's been four years," he reveals. "Which sounds like a lot."

I scoff as the glass doors automatically open, impressed and absolutely baffled. "Four years is an amazing feat, Arlo. I can only dream of making it to four years sober right now. But no sex? Don't you miss it?"

I'm in awe of his self-discipline and determination. To be so single-mindedly focused on your sobriety and not allow yourself to indulge in anything is the ultimate goal. It's admirable and another reason I am so grateful to Jenika for connecting me with Arlo.

"Hey," he says, changing the subject. "Do you mind if we detour to the hospital before dinner?"

"The hospital?" Confused by the direction change in the conversation, I give him a quick once-over. "Are you okay? Did I miss something?"

"Yeah. Yeah." A soft chuckle leaves his mouth as he shakes his head. "I should've explained that better. My foster brother had a football accident the other day and my foster siblings are all at the hospital now and asked if I could pop in."

I learn two things in that moment.

One, that Arlo was a foster kid, with a found family and a support system.

Two, I'm so incredibly jealous.

For a moment, I tell myself not to impose. That I should just go home, make myself some dinner, and go to bed, but then I think of all the reasons that caused me to relapse and all the things I lacked and lost, and I tell myself I need to do better.

*One Mississippi. Two Mississippi. Three Mississippi.*

"If you're sure they won't mind," I say with the slightest hint of excitement. "I don't really have any other plans."

Arlo offers me a soft smile, reading my loneliness like a book he's read a million times before. And I let him.

"We can go in my car and I could drive you back here after dinner?" he offers.

"I actually don't have a car," I tell him. "I usually bus it here."

"Perfect." He guides us to where he's parked his car. It's a heap of junk, which for some reason makes me feel better that I don't have one. "I can take you home later too."

The ride to the hospital is filled with nonsensical conversation that flows easily between us. I choose not to ask anything probing, and Arlo keeps the conversation flowing enough to solidify that I have found a friend in him.

"So," he starts, as we enter the hospital elevator. "Lennox, the guy who had the football accident, is deaf."

"Oh, that's okay, I know sign language."

I say it so flippantly, like it's an inconsequential tidbit of information. Like it didn't just trigger a lifetime of memories I try so very hard not to think about.

Arlo tilts his head at me, impressed and completely oblivious to how much effort it's taking for me to talk right now.

"He's deaf because of the injury," he clarifies. "But maybe, when he's settled at home and if he wants to learn, you could teach us all a few signs?"

"That sounds great. My sister is deaf, so we grew up signing." I steer the conversation away from myself and keep talking. "Is he coping with the news okay?"

"To be honest, I'm not really sure." He rubs the back of his neck, self-consciously dipping his chin to his chest as the doors open. "I haven't been here as much as I should've."

I place a hand on his shoulder and squeeze. "It's okay. You're here now."

He nods and leads us to what looks like an empty waiting room. I watch him pull out his phone and tap at the screen a few times.

Almost immediately, a nearby hospital room door opens and a man about my age steps out. He's wearing dark denim jeans and a gray t-shirt, with a look of complete heartbreak on his face when he notices me next to Arlo.

"Frankie, this is Rhys," he informs him as we get closer to the room. "He's a client at the gym."

I pretend not to be annoyed that he called me a client and not a friend, and choose for my focus to remain on whatever is going on with these two.

"The gym?" Arlo's friend, Frankie, repeats, seemingly confused.

"Yeah, I thought Clem would've told you. I run programs at the gym for..."

Arlo's eyes dart between me and Frankie, a little frazzled at having to explain exactly what the purpose of the gym is.

"For recovering addicts," I finish, without any shame. I extend my arm out, hoping it serves as some sort of olive branch. "We were going out to dinner, but Arlo wanted to make a pitstop here first. I hope you don't mind me tagging along."

"Dinner," he echoes.

*Shit. Did I just make this worse?*

He slips his hand into mine and shakes it... well, if you can call it that. Eventually, he shifts his gaze to Arlo, missing that initial warmth he seemed to walk out of the room with.

"You didn't have to stop by if you had a date."

It's obvious now these two have history, and I wonder if he's the main reason Arlo hasn't slept around in the last four years.

"We're not on a date," Arlo says firmly, his feet moving him closer to his friend and farther away from me. He clearly has a point to prove. "I don't date clients."

Frankie releases his hold on my hand and slips it into his jeans pocket. He straightens his spine, purposefully moving closer to Arlo.

I definitely feel like I'm intruding on a private moment.

"You don't date clients?" he asks Arlo.

I watch the two of them like a voyeur, but I'm finding it difficult to turn away. The tension between them is palpable; the kind you have when you love someone but you've also hurt them. They really need to fuck or fight it out.

Arlo keeps his voice even, low enough that I know it's only for his friend to hear, but not too low that I can't make out what he says.

"I don't date anyone. Ever," he says.

The air between them becomes thick and charged, suffocating me. It's apparent they've both completely forgotten I'm here.

"Arlo says it's not good for his sobriety," I pipe in, pretending that

I've been part of their conversation the whole time. "I'm hoping I can be as disciplined as he is."

My voice has the desired effect, like a pin popping a bubble.

"That's great," he says to Arlo as he puts some distance between them. "I'm so happy it's all working out for you." He turns to me. "And you too. Good on you for getting sober. I know it's not easy."

"It's not," I agree. "But Arlo helps."

I don't know their history, but it's evident it's long and deep. In the short time I've known Arlo, it's easy to see he isn't the guy who toots his own horn—you'd be hard pressed to hear him say a single nice word about himself.

But if this friend of his needs a reminder of all the ways Arlo has made a life for himself, I'm happy to be the one to list them.

Sobriety should never go unnoticed, not for someone like Arlo.

"Lennox is coming home tomorrow, so we figured we would order pizza to celebrate. I know you have plans, but you're more than welcome to stay and eat with us."

"We'd love to," I say, knowing that Arlo already regrets not being here enough with his family. I don't want to be the reason he isn't with them tonight. "Is it already ordered or would you like us to go pick it up?"

"Umm." He gestures behind me. "We waited to order, but I can ask everyone what they want and go and get it. No need to trouble yourselves."

"What if you and I go get it?" Arlo suggests.

"And leave Rhys here?"

"I don't mind," I answer, wanting these two to be alone more than I need to eat pizza or be third wheeling with strangers. "I can sit in there till you guys get back."

"No." Frankie shakes his head. He places his hand on the door handle and presses down to open it. "Let's introduce you to everyone and then we can decide what we're going to do about the pizza."

Four pairs of eyes follow the three of us as we enter the room. If anyone is surprised by the stranger that is me, they don't show it.

My eyes snag on the guy in the hospital bed, who I assume is Lennox, with his mussed-up light brown hair and chocolate-colored eyes. They're sad chocolate-colored eyes.

Sad but beautiful, and staring right back at me.

Neither one of us looks away.

I don't want to.

I don't know what compels me to do it, or why I feel like I'm in the right place at the right time in my life, but I channel my little sister, pushing past the agony of missing her, and move my hands and fingers in a way I haven't done in years. It isn't completely accurate, and each completed sign feels a little rusty.

"I know none of you know how to sign, but I wanted to say I'd be happy to teach you all," I say and sign at the same time.

Lennox's gaze finally drops from mine and to his whiteboard as he scribbles on it. When he lifts it up, I'm surprised the question is for me.

*Where and why did you learn how to sign?*

# 8

## LENNOX

Everyone's eyes are trained on Rhys's, including mine. He's like a breath of fresh air that blew into the room at just the right time.

The night had already been shaping up to be the pick-me-up that I needed. I found myself smiling and laughing despite how heavy my earlier conversation with Frankie was.

It was the first time I was in a room with more than one or two other people since the accident, and I'd be lying if I said it wasn't overwhelming. It was actually more than overwhelming; daunting was probably the word I would use. But for the first time in four years, every single member of my family was in the same room, and no matter what I was feeling internally, I didn't want to be the one to ruin that.

I tried hard not to focus on the silence, and be proactive in working out the most efficient way to communicate with everyone without falling behind or feeling left out. It was a struggle, but I'm determined.

With each hour that passed, talking became my least favorite way to communicate, almost like my brain decided if I'm not using my ears, then I'm not using my mouth either. It was a strange connection that I'm sure could be medically explained, but for now I was doing whatever felt right and comfortable.

Texting was a godsend; all of us in a group chat that left nothing unsaid, and because of that, I felt as included as possible, but when I watched all of them conversing with one another, it fucked with my head a little, that I could remember the sound of their voices but I didn't actually know what they were saying.

They tried to avoid talking in front of me, but I don't want that. I don't want them to change their whole lives and their habits for me.

I need to rewire my brain to trust that I don't need to be part of every conversation and that every conversation doesn't need to include me.

And then Rhys walked in.

Signing and talking, like it was literally no big deal.

He doesn't share the awkwardness that everybody else does. He doesn't share their concern or worry. And he isn't too bothered about hurting my feelings, and I love it.

I love that, to him, I'm just Arlo's deaf foster brother. With Rhys, it already seems that I don't come with baggage. He takes me at face value and treats me and my limitations like everyone else in the room.

Remy and Clem take turns getting Rhys to show them how to sign the letters of their names and mine and Samuel's name, and now I'm starting to worry he'll feel like a circus monkey.

"Hey," I say, using my voice for the first time tonight, feeling territorial and protective over a man I know nothing about. "Leave him alone. He isn't here to perform for you."

Clem and Remy both look at him apologetically before Clem grabs my whiteboard and quickly scribbles on it and shows it to me.

*I'm sorry. I didn't think he would mind.*

Rhys peeks at the board, shrugs, then points at the word "sorry."

He follows it up by rubbing a fist over his chest, allowing us all to put two and two together.

Remy and Clem follow his actions, apologizing to him. He just smiles, completely unbothered.

Noticing the hospital room door open, I watch Arlo and Frankie walk inside the room, pizza boxes stacked in their hands, both of them light on their feet. The sight of them at ease together, makes my chest squeeze with happiness. It's obvious whatever ended between them four years ago is far from over. They'd loved one another then, and there is no denying they still love one another now.

The stacked pizza boxes are on a spare chair at the end of my hospital bed, and when Remy opens up the first box with a huge chunk taken out of a slice, I can't help but laugh.

Rhys looks between us, and I realize we're all laughing and it's not me who's left out in this moment.

"When we were younger, whoever went to pick up the pizzas would bring them back with a huge bite taken out of one slice in every box. It became a tradition of sorts." I point at the open boxes. "As you can see, it's still going strong."

Rhys nods and laughs, or so I assume by the shake of his shoulders and widening smile. When I turn to look at Frankie, he's watching me with comfort and relief, and I'm thrilled with the idea that when he returns to Seattle, he'll be leaving without the worry he arrived with.

Over the next fifteen minutes, everyone keeps busy, feeding their stomachs and quenching their thirst. Everyone takes their time, sitting and standing, spreading themselves out across the room. They all take turns to quickly check in with each other while I just soak everything in.

Clem and Remy are the first ones to rise up from their seats and announce their departure. While Remy clears up their plates and napkins, Clem grabs the whiteboard and marker to tell me of their plans to leave.

When I read her words, I wink at her, and she bends over to kiss me on the forehead.

She then raises her hand, which is closed in a fist, and then releases her thumb, forefinger, and pinky all at the same time.

*I love you.*

I return the sign and then sneak a peek at Rhys from the corner of my eye. It was the first thing Clem asked him to teach her, and a wide smile of pride stretches across his face as he watches us sign to each other.

Clem waves to Samuel and Rhys and then makes her way to Frankie and Arlo, where I guess she's explaining the sign, because they both immediately raise their hands, telling her they love her.

The three of them laugh, and I almost want to cry from the emotional whiplash that is today. There is no way I could've ever anticipated today ending like this.

When Remy leaves, it's just Samuel and Rhys on either side of me. It feels natural, sitting with them, watching Samuel and Rhys talk like old friends. There's an ease between them that I acknowledge to be the same ease between Samuel and me when we first met.

They go back and forth with the whiteboard, the whole concept feeling more like a game, especially when we all have cell phones that make the non-verbal communication process infinitely easier.

It isn't till I notice Arlo moving closer to the bed, that I realize the three of us are not alone in the room.

Arlo places his hand on Rhys's shoulder, startling him.

They exchange a few words, and when Arlo gestures to the door, I assume he's telling him he's leaving. Disappointment rises in my chest at the thought of Rhys leaving, almost like if he goes, he'll take the lightness of the mood with him.

Samuel interrupts their conversation, and that intrigues me. Considerate as always, he grabs the whiteboard, scribbles something on it, and shows it to me.

**I'm going to drive Rhys home later.**

I nod vehemently, loving that Samuel is in tune with me and not ready to say goodnight to him either.

With all plans being settled, Arlo looks at us, eyeing the three of us with curiosity, before announcing his departure. He points at himself and then back to the door.

Understanding him, I nod and watch him raise his hand.

*I love you.*

After returning the sign, my eyes find Rhys's. It was the smallest gesture, teaching us all that tonight, maybe even inconsequential to him, but it makes my heart expand to an impossible size.

I watch as Frankie follows Arlo out the door, and I don't even think twice about whether or not he's returning. Instead, my gaze returns to Samuel and Rhys where they flank me, both looking at me expectantly.

They are the complete opposite of one another—Samuel like the sun and Rhys reminding me of the moon. They're night and day. Samuel's eyes are bright and completely transparent—what you see is what you get. While Rhys's are overshadowed by the dark circles surrounding his eyes, hiding as many secrets as I had been.

There's a pull, something tugging me to him. I can't understand it or explain it, but I recognize it. It's the same way I felt when I met Samuel.

At ease.

Familiar.

Unanticipated.

"So, your sister is deaf?" I ask, interested in more than the sliver of information he provided everyone when I asked him earlier how he knew sign language.

He doesn't seem perturbed by my questioning nor does he clam up like I expect. My legs are crossed on the bed, with Samuel up on the bed next to me and Rhys in a chair on the other side.

Rhys picks his cell up off the mattress and his fingers work across the screen. When he hands it to me, I notice the contact entry with my name on it and my number underneath. He has it from the group chat Frankie created, and from the thumbs up he's throwing my way, I assume he's checking if he's assigned the number correctly. He asks Samuel the same thing, and seconds later, it's a group chat created for just the three of us.

Forgetting to do it earlier, I now save Rhys's number into my phone and patiently wait for his message to show up.

He raises the speaker of the cell near his mouth and begins talking into it, I shift my gaze to watch Samuel's facial expressions as he takes in the information that hasn't yet reached me.

I thought it would be something that would bother me, but I'm so stupidly in love with Samuel that an excuse to stare at him is more like a prize than a problem.

Whatever Rhys is saying has a small, sad smile appearing on his face. I read the words on the screen, trying and hoping that they'll connect the dots.

> Rhys: My sister's name is Kayla and she was born deaf. She's the best thing to ever happen to me. She was an oops baby; my parents had her when I was seventeen. Let me tell you, we were all surprised by the news. My parents were so proactive when they found out and encouraged the three of us to learn how to sign together. By the time Kayla was about six months old, we knew enough to teach her the basics, and it all truly just blossomed from there. Eventually, signing became the primary way of communicating whenever Kayla was in the room.

I'm sure that if I could hear his voice, I would hear the inflection that told anyone listening just how much he loves his sister, but the anguish on his face indicates there is much more to the story.

> Me: How old is she now?

> Rhys: I'm twenty-seven and she recently turned ten.

> Me: She must love having you as an older brother.

When he doesn't respond, and I can see the rise and fall of his shoulders, I know I've unintentionally hit a sore spot.

As if reading my mind, a message comes through from Samuel.

> Samuel: Rhys, are you okay?

Instead of answering the question, Rhys pushes his chair back, away from the bed. He doesn't bring the phone to his mouth this time, keeping his head down and choosing just to text.

> Rhys: I want to be upfront with you both.

> Rhys: I'm in recovery. That's how I know Arlo.

I raise my eyes to meet his, and his gaze darts between mine and Samuel's. Almost like he's waiting for a reaction.

"Are you expecting us to throw you out of the room or light you on fire?" I ask half-jokingly.

A text comes through

> Rhys: No. *eye roll emoji*

I look down at my screen and then at Rhys, who is staring at his cell but not typing. I catch Samuel's attention, silently asking, *what do we do next?*

He shrugs, and we both patiently wait for Rhys to decide if he wants to continue the conversation, but when he doesn't show signs of it, an unexpected pit of dread sits in the bottom of my stomach, worried that the night is coming to an end.

I can't explain my interest in Rhys or the ease he has brought me in such a short amount of time, but I don't want this to be the first and last time I feel this way.

Grasping on to the only thing I think of, I anxiously send the next text.

> Me: Do you have time in your recovery to teach me sign language?

# 9
## RHYS

I can't explain why a simple sentence on my screen has my stomach filled with butterflies.

There's nothing about this night that's been even remotely predictable. Arlo left and I'm still sitting here with his foster brother and his... boyfriend?

I can't tell if they're together, but it's obvious Samuel is protective over Lennox, and Lennox is dependent on his presence. They kind of move like a well-oiled machine, Samuel knowing Lennox's needs before he even opens his mouth.

If Lennox's injury had been older, I would guess that the both of them had perfected the art of communicating without words. But I'm certain this isn't that.

I look down at the screen again and back up at Lennox, who is not so patiently waiting for me to reply.

Me: You want me to teach you to sign?

Lennox: Us. Can you teach us to sign?

I turn to Samuel, who looks completely unfazed by Lennox

making decisions for them both, reiterating the fact I haven't been completely imagining something going on between them.

> Samuel: Only if it fits into your schedule. We don't want to get in the way of your recovery.

I learned quickly that if you tell people early on you're in recovery, then you're less likely to invest your time into unsupportive relationships. It was a way to weed out the trash from your life, so to speak.

The two men in this room make me cautiously hopeful that I can maybe make friends who understand the importance of putting myself first, without thinking I'm selfish. It makes me want to lay it all out on the metaphorical table from the get-go and see where the cards may fall.

They're watching me with equal parts curiosity and patience, content with waiting for me to answer the question.

Bringing my chair back closer to Lennox's bed, I feel the knots I usually carry in my upper back slowly start to loosen. I can do this. I can be honest with them.

I find a comfortable position and just focus on getting the words out.

> Me: I've been sober for a little over three months, but I was in rehab for most of it. I started taking drugs when I was a teenager, but I finally admitted to having an addiction when I was twenty-one.

> Me: I left home to meet up with some friends and get high. I did this all the time. But this one day, I was so desperate for my next hit that I forgot I was babysitting Kayla. She was napping, and I left. Five hours later, my dad found me passed out in my friend's pool house.

The memory alone forces bile to creep up my throat, and it takes every ounce of willpower I have to keep the pizza I ate earlier from making a reappearance.

I continue typing.

> Me: He drove me home, helped me get into the shower, asked me if I wanted to eat anything, then put me to bed. He didn't say a single word about Kayla. And it wasn't until I woke up the next day that I realized she and my mother weren't home.

> Me: When I found my dad in his home office, I asked where they were. He sat there, staring at me incredulously, and at that time I didn't realize why. Like a switch flipped, he rose up off his chair and launched himself at me. And that was the last thing I remembered.

> Me: I woke up barely clinging to my life and was sent to rehab a week later.

Keeping my head down, I wait for a text from either of them, but when nothing shows up, I know I've fucked up. I've told them too much, or, as they should be, they're completely repulsed by my actions.

*One Mississippi. Two Mississippi. Three Mississippi.*

"So." It's Lennox's voice that breaks the silence. "What you're saying is your dad tried to kill you?"

When I hear his question, my throat constricts, and I'm grateful for all the technology in the world.

> Me: With reason. I left my four-year-old deaf sister alone for five hours, and I didn't even have the decency to remember it in the morning.

I leave out the part where I deserved to die, and that almost every day since, I've woken up wishing he finished the job.

"And what's your relationship like with your family now?" Samuel asks.

The text shows up in our chat with Lennox only a second later.

> Me: They pay for my housing and for every time I've needed rehab and my health insurance.

"Really?" Lennox asks incredulously.

Unable to help myself, I raise my head and look at Samuel and Lennox, who are both staring at me intently. I choose to speak into my phone this time, because I want to see their faces as I finish the story.

"My dad pays for everything so when I die from an overdose, nobody can look at him and say he didn't do everything he could to help me."

I quickly press send and then look at Samuel, whose face has completely fallen at my revelation. When I turn to Lennox, I catch him working his throat and wiping the corner of his eye. "And your sister?"

Somehow he knows the answer, but I speak into my phone and send it to him anyway.

"I'm not allowed to have a relationship with her."

———

After I drop the bomb on them about Kayla, the conversation turns light and the three of us resume talking about things that don't matter. Food, football, and how I would never love working out as much as they do.

I don't bring up teaching them sign language and figure now that I've told them everything I want them to know, they have my number and can reach out. For what it's worth, opening up to them was unlike any time I've ever rehashed that story.

Telling your story to others in recovery is easy, because they'd all hit rock bottom. But when you tell people who don't necessarily understand addiction, or maybe weren't exposed to it, the process is different.

I always feel the guilt and the shame, and for a split second, this was no different, and then I'm usually always rewarded with judgment and disgust. Truthfully, I understand those feelings. I judge and am disgusted with myself daily, but choosing to share my story with Lennox and Samuel is new and makes me feel both vulnerable and scared.

I care what they think of me.

I bask on this imaginary pedestal they put me on, and I'm not ready to be knocked off it. But as to be expected, their empathy continues to surprise me. They don't flinch and they don't judge, but they do make me hope, and that feels so dangerous.

On one hand, hope keeps you going, but on the other, nothing hurts more than the loss of it.

When Frankie returns to the hospital, Samuel and I take it as our cue to leave, and we reluctantly do so. It's clear that Samuel hates being without Lennox, and after the connection I saw between them, I understand why.

A car beeps and its headlights flash in the distance as we walk side by side through the hospital's dark parking lot. As we get closer to the car, I notice it's a fairly new Honda Civic.

"How did you score this sweet ride?" I ask.

He looks at me over the roof of the car. "My mom likes to over-compensate."

"For what? Did she run over your family pet?"

He laughs as we both climb into the car. "Something like that." Placing his cell phone in the cup holder, he points at it. "Can you please type your address in?"

I type in the details and he concentrates on backing out of the parking spot. I don't miss how he's bypassed answering my question, but I choose to let it go, out of respect for his privacy. Not everyone wants to be an open book.

Instead, my eyes take the time to gaze at his appearance. I know he and Lennox play football together, and there's no hiding the way they both fill out their clothes, but where Lennox is lean, Samuel's muscles are more defined and bulkier.

He sure is pretty to look at.

"Thank you for taking me home," I say

He chuckles. "You haven't made it there yet."

His joke catches me off guard in the best kind of way. "You're funny when you're not busy being Lennox's bodyguard."

"What's that supposed to mean?" Thankfully, his tone isn't defensive or irritated as he drives us out of the hospital parking lot and waits for my answer.

Cautiously, I choose to tell him the truth, even though I'm not sure how he'll react. With Lennox it all came easily. No matter what we spoke about, there didn't seem to be a filter between us. But I noticed Samuel was reserved, happy to shower other people with attention, as long as it stayed off him. And since he doesn't have Lennox here to distract him, I figured I'd use this opportunity to work out what they are to one another.

"I'm just saying, whatever you two have going on, seems pretty intense." I stare at his profile as he purses his lips together. "Are you together?"

Silence envelopes us, and just when I think he's going to ignore my question again, we stop at a traffic light and he answers me. "No, we're not," he says.

His answer truly surprises me. "Really?"

"Is that so hard to believe?"

"Actually, yes." I nod vehemently. "Either you two are blind, or you're both too scared to bring it up."

"Is that your professional observation?"

This makes me laugh. "Please. I have never had a single healthy relationship in my life."

"So, what makes you think we're together?"

I shrug, not wanting to sound creepy or unhinged or give away that while we spent most of the night talking, I also spent a lot of my time watching them.

"You're just so in sync with each other," I admit. "And your eyes do this thing where you follow the other's every move."

His lips lift in a smirk at my words, and I find my own mouth mirroring his. "You're totally in love with him aren't you?"

This time when the car stops, the look in his eyes and the smile, wide across his face, actually take my breath away.

"I've never told anyone that before," he breathes out, like he's relieved to share his secret.

"I hate to burst your bubble, but you didn't tell me, I guessed."

Playfully, he shoves my arm. "Shut up."

We're laughing and smiling goofily at one another, and by the time Samuel parks in my driveway, I'm convinced the night couldn't have ended any more perfectly.

Before I open the car door, I place my hand on his forearm and give it a quick squeeze. "Thank you for telling me about Lennox. It means the world that you trust me."

He shakes his head. Raising his hand to the roof, he turns the car cabin light on before shifting in his seat, his back to the driver's door. It's a small space, but surprisingly, he makes it work. "After what you told us tonight, it's me who should be thanking you for trusting me."

In therapy and NA meetings, people always thank you for sharing your story, but it never felt like this. It always seems like an expectation that in order to move forward, you need to split yourself open and let yourself bleed for others to acknowledge your suffering.

Having Samuel be grateful to have my trust makes my heart thump wildly against my chest.

As if he can sense I'm uncertain on how to respond, he initiates a conversation shift.

"I also appreciate what you did for Lenox tonight."

I look at him with confusion. "I don't know what you're talking about."

"I didn't think I would see him looking this relaxed this quickly."

"What's that got to do with me?"

"We've all been walking on eggshells around him," he explains. "Unintentionally, of course, because we've been worried. But you waltzed into that room and he couldn't take his eyes off of you."

Heat rises up my neck and my cheeks as I remember the way Lennox's eyes had locked with mine. Desperate to be liked and to fit in, I thought I'd imagined his attention on me.

Embarrassed by my reaction, I reach for the door handle, needing to get out of here as quickly as possible. Samuel just told me he was in love with Lennox, and here I am, having the most inappropriate response to someone being nice to me.

As if he can sense my internal crisis, Samuel continues. "Seriously, you were the one who changed the mood in that room tonight, and I couldn't be more grateful."

Words refuse to come together, as I try to process his compliments and my body's reactions to them. Instead, I smile and open the car door, choosing to end the night in a good place.

"Thank you for driving me home," I say.

"Any time."

I climb out of the car, and just as I close the door, Samuel rolls the window down and calls my name. "Rhys."

"Yeah?"

"Before. You asked me why my mom was over-compensating."

Interested, I lower my head into the car and lean on the window. "Yeah?"

I should tell him he doesn't owe me anything and his secrets are his, but after the relief on his face when he admitted to being in love with Samuel, I'm starting to wonder if it isn't the first of many secrets he's bottling up inside.

With his hands firm on the wheel, I know he has every intention of driving away as soon as the words leave his mouth.

I move away from the car, giving him the getaway opportunity he desires.

"She does it because she's a single mom," he says. "My dad committed suicide when I was ten."

# 10

## SAMUEL

I don't know what possessed me to tell Rhys about my dad, but I'd been thinking about dropping the bomb and driving off ever since. It wasn't entirely fair to leave him with that information and no explanation, but after he'd shared so much of himself, I felt compelled to do the same.

No... compelled isn't the right word.

I felt comfortable.

I felt comfortable enough with him to share things I have only ever told Lennox. And even the things I haven't. There is something about being in his presence that makes me feel settled, almost like he calms people down without even trying.

It's been a week since the night at the hospital, and with Lennox now temporarily living with Frankie, life for all of us, in one way or another, has resumed. It never ceases to amaze me how easy it is for life to pick right back up after tragedy.

Your heart could break.

Your life could change.

Your dad could die.

And yet everything just keeps on going.

"What are you thinking about so hard over there?"

Lennox's voice interrupts my thoughts, and I glance over at him in the passenger seat. It's obviously harder for us to talk this way, but we're improvising. I bring up Lennox's name on my car display and use the talk-to-text feature.

"Did Rhys agree to teach you sign language?"

It isn't *exactly* what I was thinking about, but it's a variation of my thought process over the last few days. Technology works its magic and Lennox reads his message.

"You mean teach *us* sign language?" he corrects

I shrug, because it doesn't really matter who Rhys is teaching, I'm not leaving Lennox's side anyway.

"What did you think of him?" Lennox asks, but instead of waiting for me to answer, he keeps talking. "I haven't been able to stop thinking about what he told us about his sister. These four years without Frankie... I just can't imagine how much he misses her."

That urge to check in with Rhys again sits in my stomach like a boulder. The three of us had exchanged a few texts over the last three days, but it was just pleasantries, a stark difference to the night we all met. I use the talk-to-text function again.

"Text him," I relay to Lennox. "See if he wants to join us this afternoon."

We're on our way to the house Lennox shares with Arlo, Clem, and Remy, to pack a few more of his essentials, because he's staying with Frankie in his rental until he moves back to Seattle. And with one arm in a sling, what is usually a one-man job, now takes two.

Or three.

It's a long shot, but something tells me he's waiting for us to make the first official-like move. He told us about his recovery from the get-go, almost expecting us to be repulsed by his flaws and want nothing to do with him.

It's naive of me to think that hadn't happened in the past, but I know it's the complete opposite to how Lennox and I felt.

A quick glance at Lennox shows him focused on his phone, hopefully texting Rhys. I wait patiently, imagining myself in Lennox's shoes as he waits for everyone to text or talk into their phone.

I have no doubt he's struggling to adjust, but like Rhys, he only focuses on the hurdle—he often forgets to acknowledge the positives; it was like that even before his accident.

"Can you pick him up from the gym?" Lennox asks.

I don't need to be told twice.

The Spot, the gym where Arlo works and Rhys trains, is another fifteen minutes past Lennox's place, but I would drive hours if I needed to.

When we arrive at the gym, I expect Rhys to meet us in the parking lot, but I'm surprised when Lennox climbs out of the car. Eagerly, I follow him, his feet moving too fast for me to ask him any questions. I reach for my cell to catch up on whatever was said in the group text, but I come up empty, having left it in the car in my haste to follow Lennox.

Walking into the gym, the smell of sweat and disinfectant permeates the air. My eyes work overtime scanning for a familiar face, but I don't see one. When my gaze finds Lennox, I'm surprised to see he's frozen.

Standing still, eyes wide.

Putting a hand on his shoulder, I try to get his attention and narrow my eyes at him in question. I can feel him trying to regulate his breathing under my touch, but no words come out to explain what he's feeling.

I give his shoulder what I hope to be a reassuring squeeze.

He scans our surroundings one more time before his gaze lands back on me.

"I haven't been anywhere but the hospital, home, and Frankie's place," he says. "I didn't realize how surreal it would be to be in a public place and not be able to hear anything."

The gym isn't at its busiest, considering most people are usually at work in the middle of the day, and for that, there couldn't really be a better time for Lennox to have this revelation. I let my hand drop from his shoulder and then slide my fingers through his. He eyes me curiously, but he doesn't shy away from my touch or drop his hand from mine.

These last few days have made me bolder in my physical affection toward Lennox. If he's noticed, he hasn't said anything.

I try to lead him to the exit, not wanting him to feel unnecessarily overwhelmed by everything around him, but he shakes his head.

"We came here for a reason," he reminds me.

I don't want to argue with him any more than I like to see him struggle to adjust, so I have to trust he knows what his limits are and when he's reached them. Slowly shifting our focus, I follow his lead and look around for Rhys, but he's nowhere to be found.

But when I look at Lennox again, his expression has changed from panicked to a little bit sheepish. His hand is still in mine, so I squeeze it expectantly.

"Okay, there's a good chance he's already left."

Confused, I raise my free hand, in a *what the fuck are you talking about* gesture, and Lennox laughs. Loud and unexpectedly. Even though I have no idea what's so funny, his laughing is contagious and I can't help but join in.

When he finally manages to catch a breath, he sighs, a smile still lingering on his face. "One minute I'm panicking, and the next you're talking to me in facial expressions and shrugs, and I understood every one," he explains, his voice holding a little bit of incredulity. "I didn't expect that. Just caught me off guard, that's all."

His cheeks are flushed as he tries to explain himself, his eyes, even just a little brighter than they have been in days. Like he just realized that maybe everything is going to be okay.

That *he* is going to be okay.

I want to kiss him.

I want to cradle his face in my hands and finally press my lips to his. I want to finally tell him how I feel about him, without saying anything at all.

But I've waited too long, and now I have to wait even longer. I have to respect the timing of it all, and everything he's dealing with. I can't assume that any time would be a perfect time. I mean, what if I've missed my one opportunity? What if I'm too late?

What if he doesn't want me anymore?

It isn't the time or the place for me to fall down this rabbit hole, so I switch gears and point to his cell phone. I hold out my hand and he places it in my palm. I search through it for the messages between him and Rhys.

> Hey. How are you? What are you doing today?

Hi! I'm good, and you? How's it been out of the hospital?

I'm at the gym, just finishing up a workout.

> I was wondering if your offer to teach us a few more signs still stands.

> We're on our way to my place to grab a few things and then heading to Frankie's place. But we're free after.

The offer definitely still stands. What's the address? I can catch the bus there when I'm done here.

> We can just pick you up. Samuel's already driving.

No, I'm fine with public transport. Give me the address.

> Nobody is fine with public transport.

I am. Address?

Shaking my head, I exit the texting app and find his notes app. Looking up at him, I bring the phone to my mouth and talk.

"And you thought the best course of action was to come here and interrupt his workout session?"

Lennox rolls his eyes at me. "Stop being so dramatic. He said he was finished." His face turns serious. "I would never interrupt a session or encourage him to ditch them. We both know how important they are. But I didn't see the point in him catching a bus when we could easily pick him up."

Lennox has a point, and I truly don't mind, but despite being the one to ask Lennox to initiate the conversation with Rhys, a part of me is filled with worry that if we push too hard, it will scare him away.

I return to speaking into the phone. "What's your plan? Are you going to stand outside the bathrooms and wait for him?"

He smirks when he reads the screen "*We* are going to stand outside the bathrooms."

I shake my head vehemently, and he laughs again. "I'm kidding. But if we stand here for a few more minutes, I'm sure we'll cross paths."

I'm about to relay another message to Lennox when he just shakes his head at me. "I don't know how I know, but to answer your question, I don't think he's left yet."

I speak into the phone anyway, our smiles matching. "So, you just know what I think now?"

"Apparently."

His gaze lingers on mine, just before we both turn to find a freshly showered Rhys, in low-hanging sweats and a t-shirt, walking across the main gym floor toward us.

The way he bites the inside of his cheek to try and hide his smile is unmissable, solidifying that we made the right decision by showing up. His cell is already in his hand, but when he looks down at the screen and starts texting while walking, I anticipate the arrival of his message.

Lennox's phone vibrates in my hand and I raise it between us to read.

> I was perfectly fine with catching the bus.

"I'm sure you are," Lennox says as Rhys reaches us. "But friends don't let friends catch the bus."

Just like the hidden smile from earlier, Rhys tries so hard to school his features to hide his reaction to Lennox calling him a friend.

It's sweet, but if he isn't going to let himself show how excited he is to see us, I hope the smiles on our faces are enough for him to know just how happy we are to see him.

I point between the two of them and tip my head to the exit door in question.

They both nod, walking ahead of me, shoulder to shoulder, catching up on whatever it is they want to share with each other.

I take my time behind them, enjoying the view, watching their ease together, hearing them both laugh. I don't care that there's no rhyme or reason as to why Rhys's well-being is important to me. The only thing that matters right now is that there is no denying that Lennox feels it too.

# 11

## LENNOX

It was becoming the new normal, everybody lazing about at Frankie's rental every night after dinner. Even though I live here too, it doesn't really feel like my house, or even ours. It feels more like an intermission, like the wait before the next part of the show.

Truth is, I don't really want to be at home, alone, while everyone else's lives go back to normal. At least with Frankie, he doesn't have anything else to do but keep me company while I find my feet.

I told myself forgiving Frankie was a necessity, that life is different now and I can't take all my abandonment issues out on my brother. But in reality, seeing him in the flesh, putting his whole life on pause for me, heals that little eight-year-old boy inside of me who was convinced nobody had ever loved or cared enough for him.

I'm sure the resentment will resurface at some point, but I'll cross that bridge when it comes instead of wasting time I don't have, anticipating something I know, no matter what, we can get through.

Clem, Remy, Rhys, Samuel, and I are all stretched out in the living room while Frankie and Arlo are busy dancing around one another in the kitchen. It was entertaining to watch at first, but now it's just frustrating as all hell witnessing the back-and-forth between them.

Clem and Remy share a recliner and I'm lying across the three-seater couch with my head practically in Samuel's lap. I'm waiting for him to move, or maybe show any signs of discomfort, but he doesn't. Not once, and I don't know why, but that fucks with my head even more.

It's hard to resist him in general, but lately, he seems to have allowed himself to be affectionate toward me, and I'm a masochist for it. I have absolutely no idea what's going on in his head, and for all I know, this is all platonic, because it could be. Frankie and Clem raised me to know that there is no hard and fast rule that says men couldn't be affectionate or show emotions with one another or that it had to mean more than face value, but my gut tells me Samuel and I are anything but platonic. The feeling is impossible to ignore, and until recently, it seemed like ignoring it is what he wanted to do.

Right now, it's almost like he's begging me to call him out on it. I want to, but everything around me seems so entangled with my accident that I'm too scared to ask questions, to dig deeper, to demand the truth.

Just like the accident brought Frankie here, maybe the accident made Samuel feel like he can't walk away from me, and knowing that could be the reason he changed his mind about us makes me feel infinitely worse.

My eyes stray to Rhys, sitting on the other recliner in the room, laughing at Remy and Clem as they argue over which fast food burger is superior. They're about ten minutes away from grabbing a pen and paper to write a pros and cons list. I'm so used to them being like this, that even without my hearing, I still know how they bicker. Like any younger brother, Remy finds extreme pleasure in annoying Clem and spends a lot of his time working out ways to get her riled up.

Usually, disagreeing with her about anything is sure to do it.

Rhys doesn't seem bothered by their antics at all. In fact, I often catch him looking at them with sad, nostalgic eyes, and I have no doubt he's thinking about his own sister and the relationship with her he doesn't have. I know firsthand how deep the ache runs when you miss your sibling, and it makes me want to hug him and fight for him all at the same time.

He fits in seamlessly with us, and I can't explain exactly why that matters to me. In the short amount of time we've spent together, I could see he is both reserved and outgoing. He was willing to share his story, but he isn't willing to share his feelings. And he is happy to help others but apprehensive about accepting help for himself.

He's a walking oxymoron—outwardly living one life while internally lying about the other.

From the things he told us and the things he hasn't, it's obvious he's scared. And I feel his fear as if it's my own.

It's the reason I can't focus on anyone's conversations. I'm not even following along with everyone in the group chats, because fear and anxiety have me in a chokehold.

Tomorrow is my first appointment with the audiologist since leaving the hospital. It's probably a week too late, but I spent the last week trying to psych myself up into going.

They aren't going to tell me anything I don't already know. It just seems like the final step in confirming my hearing is pretty much gone forever, and I don't feel in a good enough head space to deal with the finality of it all.

Right now I'm in limbo, my head in Samuel's lap, and I don't want to move. I don't want to face reality or try to work out my future. I just want to be here, where it's safe.

Where I know *he* will keep me safe.

With these people around me, I know what to expect. I know how to cope.

As if Samuel can read my thoughts, I feel his feather-light touch through my hair, coaxing me to look at him. When I tip my head up, he's glancing down at me, blue eyes full of worry. I reach up and try to smooth out the lines of concern between his brows, telling him I'm okay.

We were already so in tune with one another, but lately, he knows my thoughts and anticipates my needs before I speak them. He is the true definition of a best friend, even if to me, he will always feel like more.

My phone vibrates in my hand, bringing me back from my wayward thoughts. I bring the screen to my face and read Clem's text

> Remy and I are going to head home.

I turn, keeping my head in Samuel's lap. "I'll see you both tomorrow."

Clem speaks into her phone but keeps her eyes trained on me. I've come to realize the break in eye contact to constantly look down and text takes its toll on the conversation. It felt rude and abrupt at first, because it goes against the grain not to look at someone when you're having a conversation with them.

If losing my hearing has taught me anything, it's that change holds all the power. Change is the pinnacle of my fear, my truth, and my pain, but I also know that with change there is hope.

But hope just feels a little too hard to find these days.

Clem's message comes through

> Call us if you need anything.

"I will."

Clem and Remy stand side by side and simultaneously raise their closed fists in the air, in what's become our signature goodbye. They both release their thumb, forefinger, and pinky all at the same time.

*I love you.*

If watching them sign to me wasn't so damn sweet, their insistence to reassure me of their love would be comical.

I mirror their actions and feel that sliver of relief at having people in my life who love and care for me. Again, the thought takes me right back to Rhys, and my eyes move to him of their own volition.

He's staring back at me this time, but his eyes are more on Samuel and me than they are on the retreating Clem and Remy.

My skin pebbles as he watches us, a feeling that's entirely new and very reminiscent of the awareness I feel around Samuel. My body is heating up from the inside out as Samuel continues to brush my hair with his fingers and Rhys holds my gaze.

Needing a reprieve from something I can't quite understand, I abruptly sit up and swing my legs over the couch before standing up.

I expect Samuel to be looking at me with confusion and concern, but his eyes are filled with the same curiosity swimming in Rhys's.

"I'll be back," I announce. "I just need to check in with Frankie about something."

I don't bother waiting for a response, because there's nothing I need either of them to say. Rushing into the kitchen, I'm met with a kissing Arlo and Frankie.

"Ah, fuck, I'm sorry," I blurt out, announcing my presence.

I don't even bother waiting for their reaction and turn right back around and head back to Samuel and Rhys, who are now staring at me with concern. Rhys points at me and then his thumb, index finger, and middle finger curl in an O and then he flicks them open before returning the tip of his thumb to the point between his index and middle finger, signing the letter K.

I don't know enough sign language to have even scratched the surface yet—the use of your fingers to make letters that spell out words seems almost impossible every time I try. But every now and then Rhys will sign something, like now, and my brain would put those puzzle pieces together so damn quickly it surprised me.

"Yeah, I'm fine," I say. "I'm just thrown off because of my appointment tomorrow."

It isn't a complete lie, and it's the perfect cover-up.

Both Samuel and Rhys reach for their phones, and I put my

hands up, shaking them along with my head. "It's okay," I lie. "I just need a good night's sleep and I'll be fine."

At this, Samuel stands and speaks into his phone and brings it close to my face, since mine is still on the couch.

**Do you want us to go home?**

My shoulders fall on a loud exhale. I don't want them to leave. I'm flustered by their presence, but I'm not ready for them to go yet.

"Stay," I say, my eyes darting between the both of them. "Please."

Their faces soften in relief, almost like they aren't ready to part ways either. "I think we have ice cream," I say stupidly. "Do you guys want some?"

Before either of them answer, Samuel points toward himself and then in the direction of the kitchen, telling me he'll get the ice cream.

Nodding, I walk back to the couch and am surprised when Rhys rises off the recliner and takes a seat beside me. Close up, I can see the gradual change in his facial features since the first time I laid eyes on him. He's a little less sad, cheeks a little less hollow, skin showing off a little more color. The change in him is like watching the formation of a rainbow after a storm.

He hands me my phone, as if he's handing me my arsenal, and then proceeds to type into his.

The message shows up in our group chat and I realize we never communicate with each other outside of it. The three of us comfortable to be open and honest at all times.

His message shows up just as Samuel comes back with three empty bowls and spoons in one hand and a pint of Ben & Jerry's Chocolate Chip Cookie Dough in the other. It's my favorite.

I read the message and simultaneously move closer to Rhys, giving Samuel somewhere to sit.

Rhys: No audiology talk for the rest of the night. I'm more interested in finding out what your favorite fast-food burger is.

My palms are sweating as Frankie and I sit in the audiologist waiting room together. Samuel wanted to be here and Rhys said if I needed extra support he could easily change his plans. Between that and the steady stream of text messages from Clem, Remy and Arlo, I was overwhelmed by the support, which seems like such a privileged place to be in.

I have no expectations for how today is supposed to go, but I'm anticipating it to be some kind of turning point. After an official diagnosis, I have to make plans, adjust to changes, grieve for the things I may lose, and try to be open-minded about everything that is still left to gain.

That's the part I'm scared of.

I'd been through so much over the years, just trying to survive, just trying to feel worthy enough, but sometimes those insecurities got the better of me. Sometimes it all just feels a little too hard, and sometimes, when bouts of exhaustion hit, I really don't even want to bother.

I felt like I was forever picking myself up off the ground, trying hard to remain positive, but why does one person have to try so hard?

A pregnant lady exits one of the rooms and looks across the few faces seated in the waiting area. She glances down at her iPad and taps at the screen. The electronic buzzer the receptionist gave me vibrates against my palms.

It's my turn.

Frankie and I both rise and, as much as it pains me to do so, I put my hand out in front of Frankie to stop him from walking any farther. He tries to hide the hurt in his eyes when I turn to look at him, but he isn't quick enough.

I offer him a sad smile. "I have to do this by myself."

Despite knowing he doesn't agree with me, he nods, his feet reluctantly standing still as mine move forward. I follow the lady inside a room that is set up differently to any I've ever been in.

The heavy door closes behind us, locking us in. The walls are covered with what looks like thick soundproof padding, which I'm assuming is to ensure no external noises impact the testing.

We both take a seat, either one of us on opposite sides of the desk. The audiologist offers me a warm smile before pointing at her name badge and sliding a piece of paper across the table for me to read.

Her name is Judy, and the list in front of me is all the ways we can communicate during the appointment and asks me to pick the one that suits me the most.

I already hate everything about this, but I do my best to cooperate so I can get the hell out of here.

"Any of these options are fine," I say, pointing to the piece of paper. "Whatever is easier for you, works for me."

This answer doesn't seem to have the desired effect, and Judy's face scrunches up a little. She grabs a legal pad and then places what looks to be a cell phone on some kind of stand.

The screen is facing me and the words appear on them the instant she opens her mouth.

**Firstly, I just want to remind you, you don't need to make anyone feel comfortable when deciding on which way to communicate. You don't need to make your hearing loss easier on somebody else.**

Unintentionally she's hit the nail on the head. I often make myself more palatable to ensure nobody perceives me as different or difficult, I couldn't do that anymore.

**As you already know, the doctor has diagnosed you with sensorineural hearing loss caused by damage to your inner ear. Looking at your history, the trauma you sustained not only contributed to your hearing loss, it was combined with a genetic condition called  Pendred Syndrome. There's a likelihood you would've always lost your hearing, but not this early in your life.**

There were many things I hated about being a kid in the foster system, but this right here is the biggest blow of them all. To not know your family's medical history and be completely blindsided by the discovery, makes me hate my parents even more.

If there was any more proof I needed that I was brought into this world unloved and uncared for, this is it.

Judy scribbles on the legal pad as she continues to talk and the phone spits her words onto the screen.

**We're going to do a few different types of tests. They range in necessity and importance, but it's good to cover all bases. I've written down the names of each one.**

She points at the paper and my eyes make their way down the list.

- Air conduction thresholds
- Bone conduction
- Otoacoustic emissions

They're just like jumbled words on a page at this point, and my face must give away my confusion because Judy points at the first bullet point with her pen and then points at the phone on the stand.

**The first two are very common and will determine the percentage of hearing you have lost. The last test will be able to**

**determine your inner ear health, and that will give us an indication of whether or not anything can be done to restore some hearing in the future.**

I ignore the last line. Pretend like I didn't read it, because I'm not in the business of hoping. And especially not about this. My life is irrevocably different now, and yes, the adjustment wears on me every moment of every day, but I know enough to know it won't always feel this way.

It couldn't always be an uphill climb, could it?

For this... for *this*, I have hope.

# 12

## RHYS

We need to talk.

I read the text.
    And read it again.
    And again and again and again.

In all the years I have been trying to stay sober, my father rarely contacted me. I often tried to make amends and was almost always met with rejection. And every time I relapsed, my father found the time to remind me that he was glad he never bothered making the time to talk to me and hear my fake apologies, because in the end, I was nothing more than a waste of his time.

"Hey, man, are you okay?" Arlo's voice startles me.

I blink a few times, taking in all the gym equipment around me, then look back at him. "Sorry, I just got lost in my head there for a minute."

"You're not worried about Lennox, are you? Frankie said he'll let me know when they're home. I don't know if he'll be up for visitors tonight, but I'm sure you can text him."

Before reading my father's text I had been nothing but consumed with thoughts of Lennox at his audiologist appointment. Samuel and I spent the rest of last night trying to distract him from whatever it was that had him so scared.

Arlo isn't oblivious to the attachment that has formed between Lennox, Samuel, and me. And many times, his words of reassurance do exactly what they're supposed to and comfort me.

But right now, I'm spiraling.

I can't handle a message from my dad. Not on a good day, not on a bad day, not on a mediocre day. But he isn't someone you ignored. If I don't pander to his requests, he'll hold it over me, punish me more than his silence ever could.

I'm mid-workout and have no desire to continue. My thought process and motivation have been derailed, and I know it'll be almost impossible to find them again.

Not until I know what he wants.

"Rhys." Arlo's voice is full of worry now as he takes a seat beside me. "What is it?"

"I have to get out of here," I announce. Shooting up from the weight bench, I grab my towel and water bottle and head to the locker room.

"Rhys, wait," Arlo calls out.

My steps are harder, faster as I try to find my own space. When I round the corner, Arlo's right behind me.

"Rhys, stop."

My feet falter just as I reach my locker.

"What happened?" he asks.

Letting my head fall against the cool metal, I close my eyes and tell myself to breathe.

*One Mississippi. Two Mississippi. Three Mississippi.*

I don't want to talk to Arlo. I don't want to talk to *anyone*.

"Call Jenika," he says. "I know you don't want to. I know you want to be alone and just hope whatever it is disappears."

I both hate and feel justified in my mood that Arlo knows exactly what I'm feeling.

"Just take a minute. Call someone, or call someone later," he says. "But finish your workout. I promise you'll feel better after it."

I don't believe him, but I don't really have any other options. I'm still finding my feet and don't have anything else to do that I could positively occupy my time with.

Turning my head, I meet Arlo's brown eyes and continue counting.

*One Mississippi. Two Mississippi. Three Mississippi.*

"Does it always feel like this?" I ask. "Like you're just one life event away from everything falling down around you?"

"I want to say no, confidently. But we're all different. Our triggers are different and our healing and recovery are different." He runs a hand over the back of his neck, and I'm reminded just how far out of his comfort zone Arlo is right now, giving me advice. "You're trying, Rhys. It's the only thing that matters. Just don't stop trying."

He squeezes my shoulder before making his way to the exit. "I'll see you back out there."

It's not a question but an expectation, one I will do everything in my power to meet.

I look at my father's message one more time and then throw my phone into the locker to avoid looking at it again.

I don't need his words taunting me on my own time.

After pushing myself harder than usual, I finish my workout an hour and a half later and I'm grateful that Arlo pushed me to stay.

My muscles are heavy, my body exhausted, and my thoughts have slowed down to a manageable place. I trudge back to the showers, feeling less anxious and aggravated, thoughts of my father pushed to the background where they deserve to be for a little while longer.

I let the hot spray release what tension is left over and feel a sense of pride bloom inside my chest. It was one step. Probably small for a lot of people, but for me it was one completed step. One that I have failed so many times before.

After I dress, I take a seat back down on the bench in the locker room and retrieve my cell phone.

I type two messages.

> Dad, nice to hear from you. Tell me where and what time.

And the next to Samuel and Lennox

> Are you both free tonight?

————

It's a change of scenery tonight, and truth be told, when I sent the message, I was apprehensive to what their response would be.

Every other night it had been us at Lennox's house, with the rest of the crew coming and going as they pleased. Tonight, something told me that maybe, just like me, Lennox would want to be alone too.

The doorbell rings and nerves race through me at record speed. I enjoy spending my time with Samuel and Lennox, probably a lot more than I should, or more than made sense, but it all comes so easy with them.

Silences are comfortable

Conversations are real.

I don't try to be anything but the guy I am in front of them.

I don't hide.

I don't lie.

I don't cower.

Rubbing my clammy hands down the sides of my shorts, I open the door and see them both standing there in front of me. I'd forgotten how tall and solid they both are, the way they fill my doorway, their presence alone sending a complicated shiver down my spine.

In the past, I had never had a "type." It was more about the rush and need of something to fill that void in between hits.

But these two do something to me.

It's an unfamiliar feeling, and it bubbles beneath the surface of my skin more often than not.

I've been trying to ignore it.

They're in love with each other, and I have no business feeling anything for one man, let alone two. The whole thing has disaster written all over it.

Samuel leans against the doorjamb, wearing his UCLA hoodie and gray sweatpants, looking as content as ever with his arms across his chest, a complete contrast to the anxious man I met that night in the hospital.

Lennox's shoulders are a little slumped, the tiredness surrounding him unmissable, which makes the smile he aims my way mean even more. The fact that I know he's had a rough day and still showed up when I asked, fills me with an immense amount of gratitude.

For the both of them, for being here, in my space, and accepting me into their fold, no questions asked.

"Hey," I say with a wave.

Samuel and Lennox both tip their chins up at me, and a small chuckle leaves my mouth. Opening the front door wider, I move to the side and gesture for them to come inside. My apartment isn't exactly overflowing with space, and as both of them walk in, the place looks even smaller. The front door opens up to both my kitchen and living room area all at once, making it easy enough to navigate.

Samuel and Lennox walk toward the kitchen, each holding a plastic bag that they place on the counter. Knowing to keep my phone close to me at all times, I drag it out of my pocket and send a quick text to the group.

Me: What's in the bags?

It takes less than five seconds for both of them to look from their screens to me.

"We couldn't come to your place empty-handed," Lennox says. "It's basic manners. Especially after you said you were making dinner."

My fingers quickly fly across my screen.

> Me: Buying dinner. I said I was buying dinner. If you want me to cook, you're going to have to stick around long enough to watch me learn.

"We can do that," Lennox says casually, having absolutely no idea how much the idea of them sticking around really appeals to me.

His gaze darts around my apartment while Samuel takes three pints of Ben & Jerry's out of the grocery bags and, as if he's done it a million times before, places them in my freezer.

"Thanks for asking us over, by the way." Lennox takes the few steps to my couch and drops his body onto it in one big heap. He is as comfortable as I want him to be. "I know everyone has good intentions, but I do *not* want to sit around talking about my audiologist appointment all night."

I glance over at Samuel, my face obviously not hiding my worry, and the way he shrugs and shakes his head at me doesn't make me feel any better.

Heading to my kitchen, I open my junk drawer and pull out numerous takeout menus and head back to Lennox, with Samuel walking behind me. Despite ordering online nowadays, I absolutely despised reading a menu on my phone screen.

I drop them onto Lennox's supine form, and he picks them up and immediately starts going through them.

Enjoying the way Lennox feels comfortable enough to take up my whole couch, I anticipate that he'll move for Samuel and find myself sitting down on the floor.

When Samuel joins me, I point between him and Lennox expectantly.

Grabbing his phone, he talks into it and then the text appears in the group chat seconds later.

"He's moping and we're just going to sit here and let him."

Lennox continues to flip through the menus but doesn't pick up his phone and read Samuel's text, yet he somehow still manages to follow along with our train of thoughts.

"You don't have to include me in the messages," he says. "I'm honestly too drained to even follow along."

It's obvious he's trying to exclude himself, but doing that doesn't sit right with me. I understand his boundaries and his need to process the information he was told today in his own time, but I want to remind him that we're here for him.

Whatever way that needs to look.

"Pick something to eat," I say into my phone. "Then we'll find a movie to watch and we won't need to say a single word to each other."

When he doesn't reach for his phone, I pick it up off his chest and shove it into his face.

Unimpressed, his eyes dart across the screen and then he plucks one of the menus off his stomach and shoves it in my face. "I'm not picking the movie, though."

# 13
## LENNOX

Rhys was right.

After annihilating a ridiculous amount of Thai food, he picks the movie and, just like he promised, only a few words are exchanged between us.

It's exactly what I needed, and if I wasn't too busy being petulant about it all, I probably could have articulated myself so much better than lying on Rhys's couch, reading the closed captions on the screen like a miserable asshole. But neither of them seemed to mind.

Wanting to somehow apologize and say thank you all at the same time, I maneuver my legs off the couch, careful not to knock either Samuel or Rhys.

It's not like they can't hear or see me move around, but I choose to use the delay in them having to text me to ask what I'm doing, to awkwardly stack up the empty plates and containers on Rhys's coffee table and take them to the kitchen.

Quickly scanning the space, I work out where the trash can is and that he doesn't have a dishwasher. Just as I'm about to scrape the bits of leftover food into the bin, Rhys snatches the plate out of my grip

"I can clean a few dishes, Rhys."

He glances down at my sling, silently telling me he begs to differ. My collarbone is still broken, and healing is incredibly slow. I push myself unnecessarily to use my hand, but it's weak and ends up hurting me more than I care to admit.

Case in point.

But I hate feeling useless, and that's all I feel these days. And not because I can't hear.

It's because everything has been put on hold. I do nothing but exist. Me and my thoughts, alone almost all of the time.

Practically pouting, I make my way back to the living room and catch Samuel smiling at me as I walk past him and flop myself back on the couch.

"What are you smiling at?" I grumble, not really wanting an answer.

My phone vibrates against the coffee table, but instead of reaching for it, Samuel grabs it and hands it to me. I read his text.

> Samuel: I like it when you're in a good mood.

I scoff. "This is a good mood?"

> Samuel: Better than the last few hours.

He has a point, but I don't want to give him the satisfaction of telling him he's right. Another message from Samuel comes through.

> Samuel: I'm going to see if Rhys needs help. I'll be back with some ice cream.

I watch as he unfolds his legs and arms, pushing himself up off the floor. The sight of him continues to leave me speechless, and I have to admit, I love how completely unfazed he was by my surly attitude. The both of them, actually. They just took it in stride, content to wait for it to pass. And that's why I'm here and not with my family.

They love me. So much. But they hover, and after today's appointment, I don't have the bandwidth to deal with their hovering. My brain is overflowing with information that I'm struggling to process, and until it all makes sense, I can't sit there and deal with hundreds of questions when I don't know all the answers.

Not to mention, Frankie is still pretending he isn't licking his wounds because I shut him out. I know he's concerned, but I can't even carry the guilt I'm supposed to for keeping secrets from him; that's how heavy I feel right now.

My eyes drift to Samuel and Rhys as they laugh together in the kitchen, and my racing thoughts seem to slow down as I take in the ease in which they interact with each other. I should feel jealous at seeing Samuel so comfortable with someone else. Especially when he's so prickly and standoffish to ninety percent of the people he meets.

But with Rhys it's different.

With Rhys, Samuel talks and smiles and laughs. With Rhys, worrying about me isn't Samuel's focus, and I think I like that the best.

I watch them as they return, pints and spoons in hand. They both sit down on the floor and I shuffle myself upright. Rhys hands me the tub of cookie dough ice cream and a spoon, and I take it with my good hand. Remembering the sign for thank you, I use my free hand, ensuring it's open and flat, bring my fingertips to my chin, then move them away.

Rhys's lips stretch into a blinding smile, his eyes full of pride. He places his ice cream down on the table and picks up his cell. He then quickly types into his phone and turns it to face me as he brings his hand to his chest, stretching his fingers to look like the number five before pointing at his chest with his thumb.

*You're welcome.*

My chest tightens and my eyes sting as I try to keep the unshed tears at bay. Tears that have nothing to do with the sign language, but everything to do with the man whose face lights up at teaching it to me.

"Want to pick another movie?" I say, hoping to distract myself and him from the mixed bag of emotions I seem to be carrying with me these days.

He nods and, just like that, the heaviness from earlier has been lifted.

Just as I'm about to lie down on the couch, I realize my selfishness and stay upright. "You can both sit up here, you know?"

Samuel turns his head and eyes the couch before raising an eyebrow at me. Okay, it's probably a fraction too small for the three of us, but now that I'm out of my own head, it feels extremely obnoxious of me to take up all this space and have them sitting on the floor.

"Fine, I'll sit on the floor."

Samuel's hand finds my knee, stopping me. He rises up to his knees and then leans on the couch to prop himself up. He takes a seat beside me and then Rhys does the same, making it more than obvious they don't want me sitting on the floor.

It's a tight fit, especially as Samuel makes sure I have the most space because of my arm. "This is silly, I don't need this much space," I grumble.

Both of them ignore me, grabbing their ice cream and their cell phones and then squeezing themselves into the farthest corners of the couch. I can't help but laugh at the absurdity of it all.

We all take spoonfuls of our ice cream while Samuel multitasks and flicks through shows we could watch on Netflix.

It's a nice change of pace for the three of us, enjoying one another's company. There is no crisis, there is no sad story; it's just us.

I nudge Samuel's thigh with mine. "Let's watch this."

He stops it on *Peaky Blinders* and I turn to Rhys. "Have you met Tommy fucking Shelby?" I ask, knowing it sounds like the worst accent ever.

My thoughts are confirmed when Rhys doubles over, laughing at me. He's breathtaking when he smiles, and the ability to bear witness to it is the only thing that soothes the sting of knowing I'll never know what his laugh sounds like.

The intensity of my thoughts hits me like a ton of bricks, and I grab the remote control from Samuel to try and push it away.

*Is that what this is?*

*Am I attracted to him?*

I press play on the show and am not even a little bit surprised that Rhys is someone who has all his streaming services set to closed captions. It's always the little things with Rhys, derailing me one unsuspecting moment at a time.

Rhys puts the remaining ice cream back in the freezer and then the three of us squeeze ourselves back into position. It's not even a little bit comfortable, but I know none of us is going to be the first to complain.

Before I know it, we've almost finished season one and I can feel my eyelids getting heavier. I know I need to check in with Samuel and tell him we should leave, but I can't seem to make my mouth move or my eyes stay open. It isn't till I feel someone repeatedly nudging my good shoulder that I remember I was supposed to tell Samuel we needed to go.

I squint when the glow of a phone screen shines on my face. Slowly, I open my eyes, noting that it's Rhys who's holding the cell in front of my face. The screen reads:

**It's late. Samuel's asleep and I'm not really comfortable with him driving while he's tired.**

My eyes flick to the top of the screen and see that it's three fifteen in the morning.

"It's okay," I say, hoping I'm whispering. "The drive isn't too long."

Rhys grabs my forearm, his eyes pleading with me. He releases his hold on me and quickly types out another message.

**I'll get Samuel up and you can both sleep in my bed and I'll sleep on the couch.**

I don't want to kick him out of his bed.

Taking my silence as an answer, Rhys gets up from beside me and starts waking Samuel up, gently tapping his shoulder, and I assume from the movement of his mouth, calling his name.

Eventually, Samuel's eyes open and he's shocked to discover he's fallen asleep on the couch. He rubs a hand over his tired face before looking at me. Half asleep, his mouth moves and then he remembers and shakes his head apologetically.

That one slip changes my mood entirely, the whole day falling heavy on my shoulders, the ground like quicksand, dragging me down.

I want to go home.

"I can drive us home," I say, and Rhys lifts his phone up in the air as if he's reminding me of his earlier suggestion.

"We're not going to let you sleep on the couch in your own house."

At my words, the remaining haze of sleep lifts from Samuel's eyes and he looks between us. Rhys shows him his phone and understanding dawns on him.

I don't miss the subtle sway of his body when Samuel pushes to his feet as his eyes dart across the screen, and guilt blooms in my chest. He's been running himself ragged, staying up every night with me, driving himself home and waking up early for practice every other day of the week.

While my college life has been put on pause, he's trying to keep his ducks in a row to ensure he graduates at the end of this college year and balances life with an emotionally unstable best friend.

All of this makes me concede.

We could sleep here and get a few extra hours instead of him driving me and then himself home.

Will it be awkward? Probably.

Have Samuel and I ever slept in the same bed together? No. He's big on boundaries; boundaries that are no longer existent.

"Okay, fine." I turn to Rhys and then look back at Samuel, who is obviously too tired to deal with my indecisiveness. "But we'll get out of your hair first thing."

# 14
## SAMUEL

Lennox and I are standing on either side of Rhys's bed, just staring at each other. It's not awkward, but something isn't right. When Lennox doesn't speak, I grab my phone off the nightstand, but he shakes his head, stopping me.

"Nothing's wrong," he says, answering my unspoken question. "Well, not exactly. I just feel bad that you're so tired and he's sleeping out there alone. Isn't it ridiculous that I don't want him out there sleeping alone?"

It isn't ridiculous, because I had that exact same thought as he walked us into his room and then walked out without us. Grabbing my phone, I round the bed and sit on the edge of the mattress in front of Lennox. My body aches with exhaustion and my mind is still tired and sludgy, and maybe that's why I truly don't think before I grab his hand and slide his fingers between mine.

His eyes widen at the gesture, because the last time we were like this, he was injured and scared. This is not like that. With my gaze still on his, I bring his hand to my mouth and gently kiss the top of it. I hear the hitch in his breath and know there's no turning back now.

I let my eyes roam over him in a way that tells him exactly what I'm looking at and just how much I've always loved what I see. He is beautiful, in all the ways I never knew a man could be. Perfectly shaped lips, defined cheekbones, and eyes that have lived a thousand lives.

Soulful eyes that I want on me in *this* lifetime.

"Sammy," he whispers.

The nickname alone has me under his spell. I let go of his hand and bring both of mine up to cup his face. His tongue peeks out to wet his bottom lip, and it's like the strike of a match, igniting a flame between us.

With only instinct and the steady beat of my heart to guide me, I tilt my head to the side and move my mouth to his. Nobody knows me better than Lennox, but with his soft lips on my cautious ones, everything between us now is brand new.

Slow and deliberate, our mouths move at the perfect pace. We aren't making up for lost time and we aren't rushing into the future. We are, for once, living in this singular moment and relishing in it.

There is no rejection.

There is no accident.

There is no uncertainty.

Boldly, his tongue slips between my lips as his hand slides around to the small of my back. He brings me closer, every inch of me shamelessly hard now and pressed against him. The kiss deepens, and my tongue tangles with his. We're in complete sync, stroke for stroke, every one of my remaining secrets now his to keep.

The kiss gets slower and softer until we're nothing more than breaths of air in a quiet room.

"Sammy. Sammy. Sammy," he says softly.

I press my forehead against his and run my thumb across his lips, my touch leaving a small smile in its wake. Reluctantly, I drop my hands from his face and sit back down on the bed. Finding my phone, I pull up our text messages, the thread that's only between the two of us, the one we haven't used since meeting Rhys.

Reaching for him, I hold his hand and tug him to sit beside me, not wanting any distance between us, not anymore. I type my first message, needing to say so much to him, but certain even without the words he already knows.

> Me: I love when you say my name like that.

He looks up at me after reading, eyes shining, bottom lip trapped between his teeth. "Tell me why."

I bring the cell to my mouth, wanting to keep my eyes on him for as long as possible.

"I love that only *you* say my name that way," I say into the speaker. "Like I'm yours."

I press send on the message, my body shaking with anxiety. I did not intend for any of this to happen, but I won't take it back unless he wants me to.

"Are you?" he asks. "Mine?"

I speak my truth into the phone and send it. "I'll be whatever you want me to be."

It's not about labels, exclusivity, or propriety. For us, timing was everything, and I want him to know the way I feel about him is unconditional. I have no expectations on what this is supposed to look like or how we're supposed to be.

Leaning forward, he curls his arm around my neck and brings me to him. "I want to be able to do this"—he presses his lips to mine—"anytime I want."

I kiss him again, quick but firm, so he knows I have absolutely no issues with his request.

"We should go to sleep," he says. "I agreed to stay here so you'd get a few extra hours of rest."

At the mention of sleep, I'm reminded exactly how and why we ended up here. My cell is between us now, Lennox's arm still around my neck, both of us looking down at the screen as I type.

I don't know which words will make what I have to say make the most sense, but I know, for both Lennox's and my sake, and the trust we're building between us, I have to say something.

> Me: I can swap with him, if you're worried about him sleeping alone.

He gives his head a shake but doesn't look away from the screen. So I probe a little further.

> Me: Do you want him in here? With us?

Lennox's whole body stills, and when he still doesn't look up at me, I place two fingers under his chin and coax him to look at me.

His eyes are filled with fear and worry, as if he's confessing his greatest sin. "What does it mean if I say yes?"

I shrug but am quick to text him.

> Me: What does it mean if I say yes?

When he responds to me in text, I know he's struggling to come to terms with this new revelation.

> Lennox: Really?

> Me: Yes. Really.

> Me: I don't know what any of it means, but I'm not going to lie to you and say I don't feel it too.

When Lennox finally looks at me, his eyes are filled with trepidation. "I don't want to scare him, and I don't want to jeopardize what you and I have before it's even started."

Selfishly, I'm frustrated with the texting, and not because he can't hear, but because I don't want to break our connection. I want him to feel my sincerity and understanding, and for him to know that, in all this craziness, he isn't alone.

Tugging on his hand, I stand us both up and slam my mouth to his, talking to him in a way that leaves no room for doubts or questions. The kiss is hard and commanding, and as far as I'm concerned, he and I are unbreakable.

Rhys might think we're weird, or shy away, or not even feel the unexplainable things we feel for him, but tonight is a night full of risks I'm willing to take.

Lennox breaks the kiss, his eyes pleading with me as he presses his hand over my heart. "Please," he says. "Talk to him."

———

Careful not to scare Rhys, I leave a nervous Lennox in the bedroom and slowly walk into the living room. I'm surprised when I see the light still on and him sitting up and staring down at his phone.

"I thought you'd be asleep," I say.

His head whips up, and the lost look in his eyes shifts my mood entirely. It wasn't there before, and I want to know why it's there now. In three strides, I reach the couch and take a seat beside him. "What's wrong?"

"What are you doing up?" he asks, completely avoiding my question. "I thought you and Lennox would be tangled up in one another by now."

I know he intends for it to sound like a light-hearted joke, but a hint of jealousy is all that lands.

"Are you okay?" I ask again.

He exhales loudly. "I've been better."

"Why didn't you say something earlier?"

He lets himself fall back onto the couch, closing his eyes and tipping his head up to the ceiling. "I don't want to be that guy."

"What guy?"

"The guy who makes everything about him." He looks back at me. "I know Lennox had a big day, and I wanted to be there for him."

"You want to be there for Lennox?" I ask.

He nods, and I stand up and hold my hand out to him. "He doesn't want you sleeping out here alone."

His whole face scrunches up in confusion. "What?"

I amend my statement. "*We* don't want you sleeping out here alone."

"Am I in the Twilight Zone?" He glances at my outstretched hand. "Or are you asking me what I think you're asking me?"

"I don't know," I say, pretending to be aloof. "What are we asking you?"

"Samuel." He shakes his head at me. "I don't know if I can..."

When words fail him, I pull my hand back, feeling an unexpected sting of rejection.

"It's not that I don't... Fuck." He runs his hand over the back of his neck. "I have nothing to offer either of you."

"Don't do that," I snap. "Don't talk shit about yourself. If Lennox and I are the only ones feeling it, that's fine. If it's complicated, that's fine. If you just can't, with or without an explanation, that's fine." I lower my voice and try to tone down my anger. "But please, *do not* talk shit about yourself."

His throat bobs, and I can see the effort it takes for him to keep his emotions in check. When he returns his gaze to mine, his eyes are full of pain and regret, and his shoulders rise and fall. "I've got nothing, Samuel."

"Okay." I put my hands up, surrendering, hating how broken he looks. "I get it. I'm sorry I complicated it."

He purses his lips together, almost like he's trying to stop himself from saying more. I give him a few more seconds, hoping he knows he can tell me anything, but when the silence lingers, it gets harder to look at him so beaten down.

"I'm sorry," I say again. "I'll get Lennox and we'll leave."

Fighting the urge to look back over my shoulder, I walk away from him and back into the bedroom, to find Lennox curled up in a ball in the middle of the bed, the comforter pushed to the bottom of the mattress. A humorless chuckle leaves my mouth, because this was not the ending to the night that I had anticipated.

"Stay," Rhys says from behind me.

When I don't move or answer, I feel his hands on my back, followed by his head resting between my shoulder blades. It's less than five seconds, but my body leans into his touch immediately. Expecting him to turn right back around and leave, I'm shocked when he steps around me and walks to the other side of the bed. We're now in the same spots Lennox and I were standing in only about forty minutes earlier, except everything feels different.

"Please," he says as he sits down on the bed, making his intention very clear. "Stay."

# 15
## RHYS

A sliver of sunlight slips between the curtains, announcing the rise of the sun. Because of the handful of hours I managed to sleep, my body feels like a bag of bricks and I can barely pry my eyes open. It isn't until I attempt to move that I realize my position on the bed and that of the other two bodies in it.

Last night, I slipped in beside Lennox while Samuel slept on the other side of him. Just like the couch, our bodies filled every inch of the mattress, but it felt like our determination to be next to each other is what made the three of us fit.

This morning I wake up facing both of them: Lennox asleep on his good shoulder and Samuel's large frame wrapped around him protectively. They're beautiful together; their connection, even in sleep, effortless. It feels almost sacred to see them like this, in their most vulnerable state, but despite his injury, Lennox's hand had subtly glided under my shirt during the night and sits splayed against my stomach. It makes me feel tethered to them in a way that has my heart racing in fear and my cock hardening in excitement.

Nervously, I place my hand over his, relishing in the stillness of the morning and the warmth of his skin. I don't know what I'm doing in this bed with them, but I know I don't want to be anywhere else.

"Good morning." Lennox's croaky and unused voice breaks the silence. I drag my eyes away from our hands to find him smiling at me, all lazy and sleepy like. "I'm glad you didn't sleep on the couch by yourself."

It's all I needed to hear, and somehow he knew that.

I slide my fingers through his and squeeze, hoping he knows just how much I appreciate him and Samuel.

"Yesterday, the audiologist gave me a list of local places that teach American Sign Language," he says, completely unprompted. "She said I could learn online, but she thought it would be a good idea for me to meet other deaf people."

I happen to agree with her, but something tells me he isn't looking for a two-way conversation this morning.

"She also said my voice could change over time," he continues. "It's called a deaf accent. For some people it's so slight nobody would notice, and for others it's more obvious. Did you know that happens?"

I shake my head. I know what a deaf accent is, obviously—Kayla has one—but I didn't know hearing loss later in life affected your speech.

A shift in the mattress causes me to look behind Lennox and to Samuel, who's no longer sleeping. Half of his face is buried in the side of Lennox's neck and his blue eyes stare right at me.

If Lennox notices Samuel's awake, it doesn't deter him from sharing details of yesterday's appointment.

"She doesn't think my hearing is coming back," Lennox reveals, and this time there's no disguising the pain in his voice. "I didn't expect it to. Not really. But, fuck, it still kinda hurts."

Hearing the anguish in his voice breaks my heart, and it seems Samuel feels no different—both of us on the same wavelength, wanting to comfort him in any way possible. Without a second thought, I bring our joined hands to my lips and place a kiss on his knuckles. After last night, I'm learning how to follow my gut, and back to them is where it continues to lead me.

I watch as Samuel tightens his hold on Lennox and presses a kiss to the side of his neck, reassuring him of his presence. It's a new development between them, the blatant affection, and my stomach somersaults in excitement. I could watch them together for a lifetime and never tire of the sight of it.

The three of us lie here in silence as Lennox sifts through his thoughts, and I'm surprised when Samuel reaches for me, running his fingers down the side of my face.

Lennox's eyes track the movement, and it seems to distract him from his thoughts enough to smile at me. I don't think any of us was expecting this or even know what it is, but it's happening. I feel like a tumbleweed in the wind, flying with no direction, but knowing I couldn't stop.

The sound of my alarm clock blaring through the room startles me and pops the bubble surrounding us. Turning onto my back, I stretch to reach it and switch it off.

I'm supposed to meet Arlo for a workout and Jenika for breakfast. And after yesterday's message from my dad and the night spent with Samuel and Lennox, both of those things are high on my priority list.

But not as high as wanting to stop time and stay right here in this moment. I want it to be the three of us in a different world, waking up tangled up in one another, hands and legs, mouths and tongues, with nowhere to be and nothing else to do.

But that isn't real life, not yet anyway, and it won't be if I don't get my ass out of bed and start my day. Opening my texting app, I tell them my plans for the day.

> Me: I have a workout with Arlo and then I'm meeting with my sponsor, Jenika.

I ignore the shame that comes with my admission and swing my legs off the edge of the bed so I don't have to meet their gazes.

"You have the same sponsor as Arlo?" Lennox asks, letting me know he's read the text.

Looking over my shoulder, I nod at him.

"I know you have to go," he says, "but can I quickly use the bathroom and then we can leave you to get ready?"

I point to the bedroom door, and Lennox scoots himself off the bed and heads to the bathroom, leaving Samuel and me alone in the room. I feel the mattress move and then two hands on my shoulders, similar to the way I touched him last night.

"Promise me something," he says.

I'm not in the business of promising anyone anything, but I nod anyway.

"If whatever this is doesn't work for your sobriety, you have to let us know."

It's my biggest fear, but I know he's right. There is nothing more important than my recovery, no matter how good the idea of being wrapped up in these two men seems.

He squeezes my shoulder. "Promise me, Rhys."

Resigned that I'll eventually have to make the choice between the two, I drop my chin to my chest and answer him. "I promise."

"Thank you."

Throat clogged with so much emotion, I choose to keep my back to him as I hear him shuffle off the bed and walk out of the room. I'm playing with fire, of that I am certain. I just know I'll never regret it.

———

"Rhys," Jenika greets as I take a seat opposite her at a cafe a few doors down from the gym. "I'm so glad you called."

"How are you?" I ask her.

"I thought I was the one who asked all the questions."

I chuckle. "What? I can't care about your well-being too?"

She pauses and looks at me thoughtfully. "You're looking really good, Rhys."

My cheeks heat under her scrutiny. "What is it?"

"You couldn't even look me in the face when I met you a month ago," she states. "I can tell a lot has changed for you."

A lot has changed. I've been sober for four months, and for the first time in a long time, I have a support system. I have a daily routine, a solid foundation that makes me feel comfortable and confident to move to the next step.

The plan has always been to eventually support myself, get out from under my dad's thumb, and finally rekindle my relationship with Kayla. I have no intention of deviating from that plan, and yet my subconscious tells me I already have.

"Things have changed," I admit. "And I'm not sure if it's for the better or the worse."

The waiter interrupts my musings. "Can I get either of you anything?"

"I'll have an iced coffee," Jenika says

Hungry after my workout, I quickly glance at the small menu resting in the middle of the table. "And can I also have an iced coffee and a bagel with cream cheese?"

The waiter punches our order into the tablet before offering a warm smile and walking away.

My eyes find Jenika's, and I can tell the disruption has not impacted her ability to follow our conversation.

"What's going on?" she asks.

"Did you know Arlo didn't date anyone for four years?" I know it isn't protocol to talk about other people, but I hoped in this case Arlo wouldn't mind. "He said it helped him focus on his sobriety."

"Okay," she drawls. "Are you going to make me connect the dots, or are you going to spit out the question?"

I shrug. "I'm just curious about relationships and recovery."

"I mean"—she waves her hand in the air—"there is no hard and fast rule about it all, especially because nobody's journey is exactly the same. But the important thing to know is the difference between emotional and physical intimacy." I nod in understanding and she continues her explanation. "It's important to build on the emotional connection with someone before you develop a physical relationship, especially when sex is so often tied into addiction.

"It can prompt a relapse if your mind has always connected drugs and sex together. And for others, sex can become their new addiction. A new high to chase."

Her words not only make me feel hopeful, but her explanation isn't convoluted or misleading.

If I set myself parameters and expectations, then maybe, just once, I can have my cake and eat it too. I think back to this morning and Samuel's insistence on complete transparency, and that thought alone makes me feel a little less hopeless.

Unlike my family, I know I can talk to them, and I know, whole-heartedly they will listen.

"I got a text from my dad yesterday," I blurt out.

The shift in Jenika's demeanor is obvious, and if she was trying to hide it, she isn't doing a very good job. We discussed my triggers in our early meetups, so I know exactly why her hackles have risen.

"And?"

"He said we need to talk."

"Did you respond?"

I slowly nod, feeling shame under Jenika's stare that I don't have the strength to ignore him. But I was forever hoping that with each message exchanged, the next one would be the one where he said he forgave me; the one where he would tell me how much he loved me and missed me. Where he at least allowed me to see my sister.

"What if this time is finally the time he lets me see Kayla?" I hate the hope in my voice, when experience has shown me time and time again, he just loves to fuck with me.

"I can't tell you what to do here," she says. "He's your dad, and I know you want to make amends with him. But just like you asked me earlier about relationships, familial relationships can also be toxic and a trigger to start using again. You might want to give yourself the chance to be in a better and stronger place before you face him."

I hate how he's the asshole but it ends up being my weaknesses that are always under the microscope.

"She's ten this year," I remind Jenika, feeling nothing but regret as I think of my sister. "At this point she probably doesn't even remember me."

"Rhys," she says firmly, trying to pull me back from the proverbial edge. "It's one day at a time, remember?"

I pinch the bridge of my nose.

*One Mississippi. Two Mississippi. Three Mississippi.*

"I can't go another year without seeing her," I confess. "It'll kill me."

I didn't say those words to be dramatic, they're the absolute truth. Every day without her I die a little more inside, and he knows that. He depends on it.

In his world, he sees nothing wrong with handing me the loaded gun, because he'll always be blame-free if I'm the one to pull the trigger.

# 16

## LENNOX

Rhys: Why am I watching Peaky Blinders by myself?

Rhys: It's not nearly as entertaining when you watch it by yourself.

Samuel: You could've waited for us.

Rhys: I didn't know I'd be waiting so long in between visits.

As I lay stretched out on the couch, I can't help the smile that spreads across my face as I read the words on the screen. It's been like this for a week, the three of us exchanging text messages back and forth, filling up the hours, missing each other without ever really having to say so.

I feel someone knock my foot and I glance up to see Frankie staring at me, an inquisitive look on his face. He points at my face, and I know he's asking me what's got me looking all goofy.

"I don't know what you're talking about," I lie.

He rolls his eyes, and that has me laughing. Despite the bump in the road at the audiologist's office last week, Frankie and I are finally in a good place too. I've yet to tell him the exact details about the appointment, but I'm enjoying the fact that he's giving me time and space.

My accident has been a learning curve for all of us; it felt like it could tear us all apart at any moment, but it's turning out to be the very thing that's brought us all together.

Samuel and me included.

Even though my gut knows he feels something for me, I really never expected him to make the leap. And Rhys... Rhys is the sun after a rainy day.

My phone vibrates and I pick it up off my chest and look at the screen.

> You're smiling again.

He's sprawled out on the recliner beside me, but I deliberately stop myself from looking up at him, keeping my facial expressions neutral, and text him back.

> You should try it sometime.

> Are you going to tell me why you're so happy?

> I could, but then I would have to kill you.

> *side-eye emoji*

> Well, if you won't tell me about that, will you at least tell me about the appointment last week?

I bite the inside of my cheek, trying to hide my smile. I don't know if it's because I've had a week to mull over all the things Judy told me or because Samuel and Rhys gave me the space and security to process it in my own time, but right now, in this moment, I'm very much at peace with what the audiologist told me.

> How hard has it been for you not to ask me about it?

> That night I tried to bribe Arlo to give me Rhys's address so I could drag you out of there and make you talk to me.

Smiling at his revelation, I can't help but flick my eyes up to his as I type.

> You're ridiculous, you know that?

> I do. Now, tell me.

> There really isn't anything she told me that you don't already know.

> She did three tests. Two to check if I could hear anything, and based on those results she informed me that I have lost ninety percent of my hearing in both ears. The last test was just to see how damaged my inner ear is. Spoiler alert: the damage cannot be repaired.

I'm purposefully keeping the language light, hoping he knows there's nothing for him to worry about.

> Was that it?

Sitting up on the couch, I let out an exhale. "It wasn't anything new, Frankie. There's no misdiagnosis or misunderstanding. I was born with Pendred Syndrome. Maybe our parents gave it to me, maybe they didn't. This was always how it was going to go for me."

> How come you're suddenly okay with everything?

Taken aback by his questioning, I narrow my eyes at him. "Do you not want me to be?"

He shakes his head vehemently and types as quickly as his fingers will let him.

> That's not what I meant and you know it.

"I don't know what you want from me," I say, my tone annoyed. "My choices are wallow or don't. The only productive thing I can do is move forward. I *want* to move forward."

Frankie climbs off the recliner and comes to sit on the couch. Both of our bodies are turned to face each other, my legs crossed, his with one on the couch and the other hanging off the side. He takes hold of my shoulders and brings me in for a hug.

His arms wrap around me, and I feel the tension leave him when I hug him back.

We sit there in silence, and I realize Frankie has taken this whole thing harder than I have. I don't rush the hug or push him away. I could empathize with the brother who feels responsible for things that were out of his control, the same way he was forever empathizing with the boy who feels unloved and unwanted.

Family isn't always rational, but we do what we have to do.

Letting me go, he reluctantly pulls away and continues texting.

> I'm sorry. I keep thinking of that scared little eight-year-old boy, with only his backpack, nervously walking into the group home. And I don't ever want you to feel like that again.

We're finding our way back to each other again, learning how to live in the same world, on the same wavelength. There are going to be some teething issues as we become acquainted with the adult versions of one another.

Wanting to steer the conversation to something other than myself, I tip my chin up at him.

"So, you and Arlo? Finally get your shit together?"

Frankie can't hide his smile, or the blush in his cheeks either, but he tries to, using texting me as an excuse.

> Speaking of Arlo. He told me you asked him if I could move back home.

"Well, it didn't seem like you were going to ask him. And it's your house too," I remind him.

When we all aged out of the foster care system, the five of us moved into one house, and apart from Frankie, we all still live there.

I know he doesn't want to commit to staying in LA, especially since he's built a successful life for himself in Seattle. But I also know after everything he and I have been through this last month, and he and Arlo slowly finding their way back to each other, the decision isn't going to be an easy one.

I give his knee a reassuring squeeze. "Just tell me when you're ready to leave this rental, and I'll move back home too."

Nodding, he covers my hand with his and then raises it to his chin to sign "thank you." I couldn't see any of us attempt to sign without thinking of Rhys. He's effortlessly weaved his way into all our lives, and it's where I desperately hope he'd stay.

Frankie's hand repeatedly hits my knee.

"What?" I ask.

The message comes through almost immediately.

> There's that smile again. What are you smiling about?

Climbing up off the couch, I jokingly give him the finger. "I have no idea what you're talking about. Now, I have my first physical therapy appointment in forty minutes," I tell him, changing the subject and giving myself an out. "Can you drive me?"

———

Two hours later, the physical therapist is helping me put my arm back into the sling, and Frankie is taking notes on how I can replicate these exercises at home. He is more parent than brother, and as I navigate meeting new people in different circumstances and have to find creative ways to communicate, his presence is invaluable.

"Want to have lunch?" I ask him as we climb into his car.

Closing the doors, we both put our seat belts on and I poke around at my phone and pull up the notes app. I'm sure it's frowned upon, but I hold up the cell in between us, not too close to make it obvious, but close enough the talk-to-text feature could pick up Frankie's voice as he drives.

We go back and forth like this, me reading the screen as he speaks and then responding.

It gets easier every day, more familiar, more comfortable. I'm learning there is no right or wrong way to communicate; there is only what's right or wrong for *me.*

We pull up to a place called Cali Burgers a few doors down from the gym.

"How'd you hear of this place?" I ask him.

He points in the direction of the gym and it's safe to say he means Arlo. We take a seat and I let him order for me, because he's insistent I have to try the loaded fries.

When the server eventually returns with three burgers and three fries, I look at Frankie, questioning him. But he just smiles and tips his chin in the direction of the door at the same time Clem appears in my peripheral vision.

"What are you doing here?"

Standing, I wrap my arms around her waist as she throws hers around my neck. "I missed you," I say into her hair, and she squeezes me tighter.

She takes a seat between Frankie and me and immediately starts texting. I'm getting used to the creation of group chats for every occasion, because it ends up not just being me who needs to be included. You couldn't have a whole conversation through text messages and expect others to just sit there and wait expectantly till you're done.

> Clem: How's it been, stranger?

I leave the phone on the table and start digging into my food as Clem's texts come in like rapid fire.

> Clem: When Frankie messaged me, there was no way I could pass up an opportunity to see you.

> Clem: When are you moving back in? Because I don't like not seeing you every day.

"That depends on Frankie," I tell her. "When he moves, I move."

> Frankie: I'm thinking about it. Let's just leave it at that.

Surprisingly, Clem does, but it doesn't deter her from asking her next round of questions.

> Clem: Where are your boyfriends today? Or are they your bodyguards? I'm surprised to see you without them.

I'm taking a sip of soda when I read her text, and I nearly choke on the drink.

When I stop coughing, I glance up to see her and Frankie eyeing me, extremely amused.

"I have no idea what you're talking about," I say in between stuffing my face with fries.

> Clem: Oh, look, there's Arlo and Rhys now.

My head whips around so fast, it's embarrassing. But it's been days since I've seen him, and even if we've texted every day, I hate the way the three of us had to rush out of bed and part ways after our night together.

His face is flushed and sweaty, and when his eyes land on mine, I can feel the heat rise up into my cheeks and my mouth stretch into a smile.

I'm so fucked.

Daring to look at Frankie, I school my features. "How nice of you to invite everyone to lunch."

He laughs and then glances down at his phone. A text comes in, outside of the chat with Clem.

> Frankie: Don't think I missed the way you just smiled at him.

# 17
## SAMUEL

Walking to my car through the student parking lot, I'm surprised to see Lennox leaning against it. My mouth tilts up into a smile and my pulse quickens at his presence. I'd gotten so used to hiding my feelings from him, schooling my features, trying to keep my breathing even, that I had no idea how freeing it would feel when I didn't have to do it anymore.

I pluck my phone out of my pocket and text him.

> This is a nice surprise.

It was hard to miss how confident he's become these last few weeks. Finding out his diagnosis, surprisingly grounded him. With the right information and resources, he's now able to look to the future positively. There is no more back and forth about whether or not this is permanent, and now that they've confirmed it is, he seems to be truly thriving.

It would be silly to assume that all is right in his world; there are still days where the loss catches him off guard, where the circumstances aren't as conducive. There are days where expectation versus reality is a bitter pill to swallow, reminding him that he's still grieving the loss of his life before the accident.

Finally, I reach him and, without a care in the world, I wrap one of my arms around his torso, bringing him to me, and carefully bury my head in between his shoulder and neck. It's my favorite place to be, his pulse fluttering under my lips, his large frame somehow smaller when enveloped by mine.

He wraps his free arm around my neck and his fingers scratch the back of my head. "I missed you."

I move my mouth up his neck, across his jaw, and press my lips to his. I feel my whole body melt. I indulge in the feel of his mouth against mine, loving how I'm no longer *secretly* pining over my best friend.

*I missed you too.*

"I spent the day at the university student office," Lennox tells me as he leans back against the car again. "I don't like that I'll be here next year without you."

Bit by bit, Lennox is making changes throughout his life to adjust to his hearing loss. This included deferring the rest of our final semester and coming back for it next year.

Holding on to him by the loop of his jeans, I use my other hand to text him and ask him about his day.

> Do you feel better now that you can cross that off your list?

He runs a hand over his face after he reads my message. "I like that I don't have it hanging over my head. It gives me time to work out who I am as a deaf man." He tips his head to the side. "Is it weird hearing me refer to myself as a deaf man?"

> Is it weird for you?

"It was weird being in the Center for Accessible Education Office and realizing that I had absolutely no clue on how hard it is for people with disabilities to access services. How much paperwork there is, how many roadblocks." He shakes his head, his face etched with disappointment. "And what about all the people who don't have access to assistance of any kind?"

I'd found myself having the same thoughts after Lennox's accident. Watching how people interacted with him now; people who knew him before the accident and people who have only met him after. It was amazing to see that for every empathetic person out there, there was another person who truly felt inconvenienced by other people's disabilities.

I wonder if I've ever made anybody with a disability uncomfortable.

> It's a learning curve. For all of us.

I remind him.

He nods half a dozen times. "I know, I know. How was your day?"

> Obviously better now. What are you doing for the rest of the day?

That earns me a lopsided grin. "I was hoping to hang out at your place while you shower, then maybe check in with Rhys."

I love the sound of that.

Retrieving my keys from my bag, I press the fob to unlock the car and open Lennox's door for him. After he climbs in, I round the front and hop in, setting my cell on the phone stand and opening it up to the notes app. I hit the microphone and start talking.

"Have you spoken to Rhys today?"

The words appear on the screen, and Lennox answers.

"After his morning session with Arlo. He said he also had a few job leads he wanted to follow up on, but you know how he clams up when talking about it."

One night when we were having dinner with Frankie and Arlo, Arlo mentioned how there was still a lot of shame and stigma when it came to "finding your feet," and I'd wondered if it was the same for Rhys.

I knew from the conversation he and I had that night, he believes he has nothing to give. He's always so hard on himself, and he expected everybody else to be that way with him too.

"I'll text him and see if he wants to do something tonight," Lennox says as I turn off the engine.

I don't normally need my car to make my way around campus, but every now and then I'm a little too lazy to walk my ass home after training.

Side by side we walk up the three flights of stairs to my dorm room. It's not much, but it's a single—the only saving grace. When we both step over the threshold, the air suddenly feels a little too thick and the space much too small.

We've been here a hundred times together, but we have yet to be alone together since that night at Rhys's house. We were either with a group of people or with Rhys, and what we have with Rhys is intimate, but it's a different kind of intimacy.

It's more on the slow and steady, heavy on the emotional.

The lock of the door echoes around the room, and my body reacts to it like a starting pistol. My hands and mouth can't get to him quickly enough. Careful of his collarbone, I press him up against the door as gently as I can manage.

My lips fuse to his, full of longing and desperation and a crazy rush of excitement. It doesn't matter how many times my mouth has touched his, the freedom to be able to do so makes my dick impossibly hard. I'd been a stupid fool, trying to tell myself that I didn't need this.

That I didn't need *him*.

Before I met Lennox, I had only ever been with girls. Nothing serious, but never anything to make me doubt my sexuality. I lost my virginity on prom night like ninety-nine percent of boys my age. I didn't overthink it, and it wasn't mind-blowing or anything special.

But with Lennox, kissing alone makes me feel like I'm on top of the world. Like I could be anyone and do anything as long as his mouth never left mine.

"Sammy. Sammy. Sammy," Lennox says in between kisses, knowing very well just how crazy it makes me.

"I've only got one good arm," he says. "So you're going to have to listen and do everything I say."

My mouth makes its way down the side of his neck, licking and sucking, as I listen and wait for his instructions.

"Pull my cock out."

I drag my hand down his chest and then boldly unbutton his jeans. I shove them down to mid-thigh and then run the heel of my hand up and down his hard length.

"I didn't say you could tease me," he pants.

Pressing my lips to his, I let my tongue sweep the inside of his mouth, tasting his desire. Without further instruction, I push down his boxer briefs, tucking the material behind his balls, his cock standing to attention in my hand.

His skin is hot, his length heavy and hard. I let my gaze drop down to his dick and then back up to his face.

His eyes are burning with lust while our kiss glistens on his lips.

My hand moves up and down his cock, stroking it as if it were my own, just the way I like it. I squeeze the head, making him hiss, and pre-cum decorates my fingertips.

"Now it's your turn," he breathes. "Show me yours now that I've shown you mine."

I'm like a fumbling virgin, shoving down my sweats and briefs at the same time. I feel like I'm about to explode, and he hasn't even touched me.

"Kiss me," he demands.

Pressing myself to him, my mouth melds to his just as he uses his free hand to bring our cocks together. A loud groan leaves my mouth as he wraps his big hand around us and starts stroking.

The kiss turns frantic as he expertly brings me to the brink and back again.

"I want you to come, Sammy baby."

Over and over, he stops and starts. Fast strokes, slow strokes. Soft strokes, rough strokes.

My body begins to tremble as heat curls around the base of my spine.

"Fuck. Fuck. Fuck," I chant to myself.

"Come," he commands.

My mouth falters, but my body obeys. My head falls onto his shoulder, my breathing ragged, as his touch intensifies and my arousal reaches uncharted levels.

We both shudder, orgasms ripping through us, and we come, spilling all over Lennox's hand.

Heavy breathing fills the air as we both just stare at the mess we made. Sticky and filthy, and yet the sight is still so beautiful.

Tilting my head up, I'm met with eyes and a smile that are practically shining in the afterglow. He brings his cum-covered fingers up to my mouth, and I lick them clean.

Sticky and filthy, and yet still so beautiful.

"How was that?" Lennox asks, and I raise a knowing eyebrow at him. He just single-handedly blew my mind and he knows it.

I move my mouth from his fingers to his lips, sliding my tongue along his, wanting him to taste us.

His chest rumbles with a groan, and my cock somehow manages to stir again.

*Jesus fucking Christ. Tell me, Lennox, how was it?*

Sticky and filthy, and yet still so beautiful.

# 18

## RHYS

Samuel: Are we still on for tonight?

Me: Of course. Just don't be late.

Lennox: Wouldn't dream of it.

Me: Better yet, come earlier.

Grabbing a fresh towel from my pile of folded laundry, I head to the bathroom and indulge in a nice hot shower, washing off the stink and the sweat of the day, as I wait for Samuel and Lennox to arrive.

We've gotten into a nice little routine over the weeks, and my place has become our refuge. There are fewer questions and more privacy, and since we're still navigating something so new, it's become an unspoken need to not have everybody's prying eyes on us.

The cat is out of the bag when it comes to Samuel and Lennox, and as expected, nobody was even a little bit surprised. They are effortless together, and if I let my insecurities get the better of me, I scold myself at thinking I could be part of anything so perfect.

But then the days end and the nights are ours, and the only thing that matters is the three of us holding each other, letting our deepest, darkest secrets flow in the dark and helping each other let go of them in the light.

My shower ends a little too quickly when I hear my cell phone vibrate on the bathroom counter. Expecting it to be Samuel or even Arlo, I poke my head out to peek at the screen and both my body and my mind come to a screeching halt when I see my dad's name flashing before me.

He had yet to respond to my text from the other day asking when and where he wanted to meet, and if I wasn't so desperate for information on my sister, I would take Jenika's not so subtle advice to decline the call and be done with him.

*One Mississippi. Two Mississippi. Three Mississippi.*

Surprising myself, I choose to finish my shower. My father is the type of man who refuses to call people more than once. His overinflated ego makes him think that if you don't answer straight away, you aren't worth his time.

So, instead of rushing for him, I take my time under the hot spray, and by the time I'm finished, I've convinced myself to call him tomorrow, when I'm without Lennox and Samuel and there was every chance he would ruin my mood.

An hour later there's a knock on my door, and it takes every ounce of restraint I have not to run to answer it.

When I open it, my whole body sighs in relief. I hate being away from them. An hour, a day, a week, it all feels the same. It all feels too long.

"Hello," I say, whilst saluting Lennox, which is the way to greet someone when using sign language. "Come in."

I gesture inside and they both walk past me and straight to the kitchen.

"How do you feel about cooking?" Lennox asks.

I pull my phone out of my pocket and quickly answer him.

> Me: Depends. Am I cooking or am I watching you two do it?

> Me: Because I could definitely get behind watching.

Samuel chuckles when he reads my text and Lennox just eyes me, a hint of mischief in his expression.

"You could, you know," he says, with the slightest hint of seduction in his tone. "Watch us."

All the blood in my body heads straight for my dick as an image of them, naked and together, flashes through my mind.

None of us had made any concrete rules about the physical affection between the three of us, but I know they're waiting for me to make the first move. My comfort, my sobriety, my choices... they all matter to Samuel and Lennox.

I, as a person, with my own wants and needs, matter to them.

When I don't answer, Lennox pushes a little. "Cat got your tongue?"

Shaking my head, I bite back the smile threatening to spread across my face and focus back on my phone.

> Me: Maybe that can be on the menu for dessert?

My heart pounds as I press send.

The silence is heavy, and when neither of them respond, I find the courage to raise my head and look at them.

Samuel is the first to move, and before I know it, he's standing in front of me. He curls his hand around my hip and lowers his mouth to my ear and whispers, "Whatever you want is yours."

Goose bumps cover my skin at his words. We almost never speak in front of each other without including Lennox, and when my eyes search for his, and I take in the tongue that skates across his lip, the rise and fall of his chest, and the hooded look in his eyes, I know this time hearing the words doesn't matter.

He's right here with us, on the very same page.

Needing him close, I hold out my hand to him. He slips his fingers between mine and sidles up next to Samuel. Allowing their closeness to fuel me, I lean my head toward Lennox, my intention clear. He closes the distance between us, and his mouth lands on mine. It's gentle and reverent, two things I don't feel like I deserve.

As if he can read my mind, Samuel's hand on my hip tightens in encouragement, almost like he's giving me permission—and not because Lennox is his, but because this kiss is *mine.*

Shifting slightly, I lean farther into Lennox and bring both of my hands to his face. Deepening the kiss, I take what he's offering and tell myself to enjoy the way this feels. For the first time in the longest time, my reality is better than anything any dream could muster.

I relish in the warmth of him.

I relish in the taste of him.

I relish in the fact that in the morning, he'll still be here and I'll still remember.

Without even realizing he moved, I feel Samuel behind me, his front pressed to my back, his hands now wrapped around my waist, his lips peppering kisses to the nape of my neck. It's sensory over-load, but there is nothing in the world that could make me ask him to stop.

Samuel's thick length brushes up against my ass, and my own cock struggles against the zipper of my jeans. I want to stay in this exact moment, and I want to move us to the bedroom and let our bodies lead the way, but I know I need to take it slow.

Enjoy the build up.

Respect the pace.

Listen to the needs of my sobriety.

Letting my hands drop from Lennox's face, I link my fingers with theirs and lead us to the bedroom. Guiding us to the bed, I selfishly take the middle and both men find their way to either side of me. The light outside of the bedroom is the only one on and it gives just enough glow for me to see them and their faces as they both look down on me.

Lennox's hand lands on my stomach as Samuel lowers his head and presses his lips to mine. His kiss is more hungry, more impatient, like all the waiting has made him ravenous. Where Lennox's mouth gave, Samuel's mouth takes, and I will forever be content to be whatever they need me to be.

I feel Lennox's hand move down my torso as Samuel's tongue dances deliciously with mine. Fingers stop at the button on my jeans as he brings his mouth to my ear.

"Tell me what you want," he murmurs. "I can touch you. I can suck you. I can fuck you too."

I know Samuel can hear him, because he groans at Lennox's offerings, and the sound reverberates between us.

Grabbing his hand, I place it on my dick and he wastes no time pulling me out of the confines of my pants and wrapping his hand around my cock.

I'm not ready to feel more than this. I feel that slippery slope and know just how easy it would be to become addicted to this feeling. There is a difference between giving and receiving, and I am determined to master the art of giving.

Reluctantly, I pull my mouth away from Samuel's and meet his gaze.

"What is it?" he asks, a hint of concern in his voice.

"I want what I was offered," I say, trying to play it cool. I point between him and Lennox. "Let me watch."

At this, Samuel leans over me and captures Lennox's mouth. I replace Lennox's hand with mine and then I shift up the bed till I'm seated upright against the headboard, and I watch the beauty that is them.

They close the distance between one another, both of them kneeling on the mattress. Their lips fuse together and their hands search for skin.

I begin stroking up and down my shaft languidly, lazily, slow enough to want to make this moment stretch out all night.

"Lie down," Lennox orders Samuel, and my dick jerks in my hand at this side of both of them I've never seen before. Samuel isn't the protective bodyguard in the bedroom; he listens to each and every one of Lennox's instructions like a good fucking boy.

I watch him take his clothes off, the lines and curves and dips of his body never ceasing to amaze me. Sitting down on the edge of the bed, he strokes himself, my own hand matching the rhythm.

Lennox walks around the bed, commanding the room even when he kneels before him. Looking up, he licks his lips and then replaces Samuel's hand with his, stroking up and down.

I take in Samuel's heavy breathing, the rise and fall of his chest, and the tensing of his stomach as Lennox expertly rolls his wrist up and down Samuel's length.

He uses his thumb to collect pre-cum from Samuel's leaking slit and then slips his thumb inside his mouth.

These two are going to kill me.

I squeeze my own cock, trying to stave off my release as I watch Lennox slide his beautiful lips around the head of Samuel's cock.

"Ah fuck," Samuel breathes out.

Lennox's mouth moves up and down, pushing Samuel's cock in farther on every glide. His gag reflex is non-existent and the thought of pushing my dick down to the back of his throat makes spilling in my hand more imminent.

He tortures our poor boy, rolling his balls, sucking on his sac, bringing him so close to the edge only to stop it all at once.

My own hand moves faster, and when I notice Lennox pressing a palm to his own cock, I quickly climb off the bed, dick in hand, and kneel behind him.

He only falters for a second, but as my mouth kisses the back of his neck and I wrap one hand around his length and the other on mine, he figures it out.

He works Samuel over. Deeper. Faster.

I continue to kiss and lick the nape of his neck, nipping at his skin every time I come close to release. And when Lennox's hips rock back and forth, his cock fucking my fist, I know we're all right where we need to be.

"Come," Lennox demands. "Fucking hell, *please* come."

The uninhibited desperation in his voice pushes all of us over the edge, and a collective moan, followed by a flurry of irregular panting, echoes through the room.

Unable to stop myself, I keep kissing Lennox's neck while watching Samuel in all his sated glory. It doesn't matter that both my hands are sticky with cum or that I can't logistically work out how to release my hold on both of us without making a complete mess.

I'm exactly where I want to be. With them both, I'm always exactly where I want to be.

# 19
## RHYS

"Rhys."

The sound of my name stirs me from my sleep, but not enough to open my eyes and respond.

"Rhys," Samuel repeats. "Rhys."

"What?" I grunt.

"Your phone."

*My phone?*

"It won't stop vibrating."

I'm certain I don't have my alarm on today. I've slowly started to give myself permission to take the weekends off.

Apparently moving too slowly for him, Samuel climbs over my back and plucks it off the nightstand.

"It says Dad."

At that, I pop my head out from underneath my pillow. "Are you sure?"

"Here." He shoves the phone in my face, and as my mind finally plays catch-up, bile rises up my throat.

He never calls back.

Throwing back the covers, I climb out of the bed, completely naked, and snatch my phone out of Samuel's hand. He flinches and I regret it immediately.

"I'm sorry," I say and sign, a fist on my chest rotating clockwise, when I notice Lennox looking at me.

"Do you want us to leave?" Lennox asks.

I shake my head just as my phone vibrates again.

"I have to get this," I say, pointing at the phone. "I'll be right back."

I practically jog out of my bedroom as I swipe at the screen. "Dad. Hey."

"You know every time you don't answer the phone I just imagine you dead in a ditch somewhere."

Standing in the kitchen, I pinch the bridge of my nose and let out an exasperated sigh. Awesome. We're off to a great start.

"I'm sorry," I was asleep.

"And yesterday?" he prompts. "Have you been asleep this whole time? Nobody sleeps that long if they're not coming down from something."

"I'm not coming down from anything," I say sternly.

"Don't use that tone with me."

*One Mississippi. Two Mississippi. Three Mississippi.*

"Dad," I say, keeping my tone neutral. "You said you needed to talk to me."

"Well, I'm not going to talk about it over the phone."

Nothing could ever be straightforward with him. If he isn't berating me, he's making me work for every fucking morsel of information he has over me.

"What's it about?"

I don't know why I ask. I know the answer, and it's only going to make me want to come out of my skin while waiting to speak to him.

"Don't be so obtuse, you know there's only one reason we still talk to you."

Ignoring the insult, I focus more on the matter of importance. "Is she okay?"

"Of course she is. She's perfect," he says, his voice full of adoration.

The tension in my shoulders lessens, only a little, knowing that she's okay. The rest of my coiled muscles are reserved for whatever surprise he wants to throw my way.

"Can we meet at The Spot? It's the gym I train at." My request is met with nothing but silence. "We won't actually be talking in the gym," I clarify. "There's a coffee shop nearby where we could probably sit and talk."

"That's fine. I'll be out of town this coming week, so how does the following Friday sound?"

Motherfucker is going to make me wait another week. "Yeah, that works." I swallow hard before asking the next question, knowing my mother doesn't take a single breath without his permission. "Are Mom and Kayla coming with you?"

He chuckles. Fucking chuckles. "Neither of them will get a kick out of seeing you slumming it."

"I'm not slum—" I cut myself off, shaking my head. Why do I keep trying to prove myself to him? We get nowhere. Every. Damn. Time. "Okay, I've got to go. I'll text you the address for Friday."

"Three p.m. Rhys, don't be late."

It's all he says before hanging up.

With my eyes closed, I tip my head up to the ceiling and take in a lungful of air.

In with the good.

Out with the bad.

"Are you okay?"

I rub my hand over my face before facing one or both of them. I don't want his negativity to touch them. I don't want to talk about him. I don't want him to ruin any more good things in my life.

Turning around, I muster a fake smile. Samuel is the only one in the room with me, and I know the second he sees right through me.

"Yeah," I say, feigning enthusiasm. "He was just calling to check in."

Wordlessly, he walks toward me with nothing but sincerity and empathy in his eyes, and it makes me want to break down in his arms.

He grabs my face, his touch gentle yet firm. "Whatever it is, we can handle it." His eyes dart between mine, searching for my secret. "We can handle it together."

Finding it impossible to say anything, I wrap my hand around his wrist and lead him back to the bedroom. Like a little kid who just wants to hide from the world, I climb back into the bed. Starting at the bottom, I crawl under the bedding until my head peeks out, right beside Lennox.

There's a hint of sadness in his eyes and I know it's for me. But I try to will it away by dropping a kiss to the tip of his nose.

"Are you okay?" he asks me.

I kiss his nose again and let him know the only thing I care about right now is being in this bed with him. With *them*. I feel Samuel come up behind me. He throws his arm over my middle and Lennox reaches for him, cocooning me in. We lie like this till they both fall back asleep, and I pray to a god that might exist, that I don't fuck this thing up.

———

"Have you ever thought about teaching sign language?"

I don't know why Lennox's question makes me pause for longer than necessary, but for some reason it stumps me. *Why haven't I ever thought about teaching sign language?*

"You've been teaching us for just over a month now anyway."

I glance down at the booklets and laptop strewn around my four by four dining table and search for my cell, but when I come up empty, I find a pen and write on a scrap of paper, showing Lennox.

*Do you think I could do it?*

He rolls his eyes. "No, I suggested it for no good reason at all." He moves a few of the papers around. "I'm just saying, I know you're starting your job at the gym this week, but, and correct me if I'm wrong, that's not your forever thing."

I don't typically think too far ahead in the future, but I know enough about myself to know Lennox is right. My job at the gym is temporary. It's more like an agreement between friends; a favor of sorts.

The place has been a lifeline, but I don't love it the same way someone like Arlo does. But the idea of teaching sign language? That makes me want to think of the future.

"Maybe these places have teaching courses," Lennox says. "You could always come with me and ask."

It's the beginning of a new week, and while Samuel is at school, Lennox and I are coincidentally discussing the pros and cons of me teaching him American Sign Language before his last physical therapy appointment.

He is firmly for and I'm firmly against.

"So you'll consider teaching others, but you won't teach me."

I huff as I bring my hand up to my ear and pretend it's a phone and then shake my index finger, asking him if he knows where my phone is.

He looks around the table but ends up grabbing his and handing it to me.

I talk into the phone, explaining my side of the argument. **"I will always teach you what I know, but you also need to be taught by a professional. And you need to meet other people, find who you are after the incident."** Then I show him the screen.

"I'm not good at making new friends," he says, practically pouting.

I continue to talk, and he continues to read. **"You'll benefit from**

**meeting other deaf people. Trust me when I say that. I think my recovery this time is different because I met people like Arlo and fit something like The Spot into my daily schedule."**

There is something to be said about being around people who have lived the same experiences as you.

It's why people like Jenika exist and groups like Alcoholics Anonymous and Narcotics Anonymous have such high success rates. There is power and positivity in numbers. But we often forget that as we trudge through our everyday struggles, that our experiences are not solitary or unique. Somewhere else in the world, someone else had that exact same thought, cried for that exact same reason, and wanted to give up on life the same number of times as you.

It's taken me so long to acknowledge this that, now that I have, I can finally see and appreciate the support system around me. I can finally see myself as a man who might want a career one day. A man who might want two men instead of one. A man who is no longer living in the past and who's just enjoying the present.

Caught up thinking, I talk into Lennox's phone and he waits for me to show him the screen.

**"Can I use your laptop, please?"**

Disgusted that I even asked, Lennox hands it to me and then stands up from his chair and walks around the table until he's seated beside me.

He watches me as I pull up different pages and read through a wealth of information about teaching ASL. When I turn to face him, anxiety has me shrugging expectantly.

"Nothing," he says, grinning and holding his hands up in surrender. And then he leans forward and kisses my cheek. "Excitement just looks really good on you."

My fingers still on the keyboard, overwhelmed by his compliment, by his observation, by the whole entire mood, I bring my hand to my chin, signing "thank you."

He winks and then bends down to kiss me again, but this time I can't help but inhale his entire presence. With my mouth still on his,

I scoot my chair back and tug Lennox off his. I guide him to straddle me and feel my cock stir when he lazily slips his tongue between my lips.

Kissing has never felt so good. I could sit here with Lennox in my lap, my mouth on his, and be wholeheartedly content for the rest of my days.

After the weekend, there's no denying there is something between the three of us. It was instant and unexpected. It's emotional and it's physical, and most importantly it's effortless.

None of us question what it is or where it's going. We don't need rules and don't require labels. There is no jealousy, no comparison, and no envy.

It's the healthiest relationship in my life to date, which makes me more determined to keep my father as far away from it as possible. As the days close in on our meeting, my anxiety plays peek-a-boo; intrusive thoughts finding me at the most inopportune times.

Lennox's thickening erection interrupts my wayward thoughts, and I couldn't be more grateful for the distraction. Slipping my hands underneath his t-shirt, I push the material up his chest and regretfully stop kissing him as I drag it up and over his head. My eyes slide over his lean chest while my hands and fingers dance over him, touching his skin, counting his ribs, and my lips dutifully follow.

My gaze finds his as I let my tongue glide over his nipple, licking and biting it before my lips settle on his collarbone. It's no longer bruised or broken, and even though his mobility is a little slow, I'm grateful the healing has happened. My mouth continues the journey, up the side of his neck, along his jaw, and ending at his parted lips, wet and waiting for me.

Gripping the back of my neck, Lennox keeps me in place as he fights me for dominance one lick and taste at a time. My cock is hard and desperate as he rocks against me roughly.

He loves being in control. I noticed it when he was with Samuel, and I can feel the fight in his every touch to take it right now.

Samuel couldn't give it up to him any faster and it was a sight to see. And for the most part, I have no problem giving it up to him either, but there is a part of me that wants to see if I can derail him, whether he'd let me succeed, and just how beautiful it would be to see how desperate I could make him.

Raising my arm, I run my hand down his forearm and up his shoulder. It's a little awkward and not the exact angle to get the message across but I try anyway, waiting to see if he notices.

I repeat the movement once, twice, and on the third time, his lips falter.

"Are you signing right now?" he asks incredulously. "You are, aren't you? Asking me to slow down. It's slow down, isn't it?" He cocks his head to the side like he's flicking through his own ASL memory cards. "Yeah, it's slow down."

My smile widens and my heart beats wildly for this man who just realized that I can still talk to him during sex.

"But wait, why do you want me to slow down?"

Chuckling, I take his chin between my fingers and dip his head down so I can capture his lips, then I stand us both up and turn him around.

He catches on quickly, and when I press down on the middle of his back, he bends for me beautifully.

My lips make their way down the knobs of his spine and to the two dimples right above the waistband of his pants. I shove them down, exposing his round, toned ass, and I can't help but take a bite. He hisses but doesn't push me away as I let my tongue soothe the pain. I do this a few more times as I bring my finger to his lips, my request very clear.

I thrust it in and out of his mouth, getting it nice and wet, as I pull one of his ass cheeks to the side, exposing his pretty hole. My own cock throbs as I circle him with the wet finger and then gently push the digit inside him. It's just the tip, almost like a little plug, just enough for him to feel the anticipation of being full.

"Oh fuck."

I lower my mouth to his hole, licking around my finger before sliding it out and replacing it with my tongue. He drops his head to the table with a loud thump and I lick him again.

And again.

And again.

And again.

"Fuck. Rhys," he whimpers. "Fuck. Fuck. Fuck."

Using two hands, I stretch him wider, pushing my tongue deeper, in and out, just to hear the way his panting and begging echo around the room.

I watch as he grabs his cock and begins stroking himself, desperately, wishing we had a thousand more hands to be able to touch every inch of each other at all times.

I alternate between my tongue and the tip of my finger as unintelligible sounds leave his mouth. I know he's only seconds away from losing himself completely, and pride makes my cock throb.

In one swift move, I turn him around to face me and point to my mouth. I open up and he slides his slick length in between my lips and his cum immediately explodes along my tongue.

I indulge in the taste of him as his hands rest on my shoulders, trying to steady himself before his body collapses into euphoric exhaustion.

"Holy fuck," he breathes out. "I think you killed me."

*No*, I think to myself. *I think I just worked out how to make you give up control.*

# 20

## LENNOX

It's been almost six weeks since my accident, and to describe it as a roller-coaster ride would be the understatement of the century. So much has happened, in almost every aspect of my life, that I was simultaneously experiencing the highest of highs and lowest of lows.

And some days it's difficult to muddle through the two.

For one, I'm no longer Lennox York, the twenty-two-year-old college student on a football scholarship. I'm now Lennox York, former UCLA student, with no job, no scholarship, a collarbone break that is finally healed, and I recently lost my hearing.

That's right, I'm deaf.

I could stomach saying that now.

I feel the loss differently on different days, but I move closer and closer to the acceptance stage every day. And it isn't because I'm resilient, or strong, or adaptable.

It's because of every single person who rallied around me after the fact. It's remembering all those shitty foster homes, remembering the neglect, the physical abuse, and knowing that if I lost my hearing then, without a doubt, I would not be here today.

I find myself putting one foot in front of the other for the eight-year-old boy who found hope when he was reunited with his brother, or because of him, I'm not too sure. But I know I didn't endure those years of hell just to throw the towel in now.

My phone vibrates on my lap and I see a message from Rhys.

> Rhys: How are you feeling?

I shift in my seat and turn to face him in the back seat of Samuel's car. My gaze bounces between the two of them. "I'm fine. It's a meetup for deaf people, not a firing squad. You're both acting more like parents than boyfriends."

The last word slips out, and I can tell from the way Samuel glances between me and the rearview mirror, the cab of the car is not just quiet because I can't hear.

Samuel reaches for his cell and presses the talk-to-text feature. My eyes almost don't even want to move to the screen, scared of what he might say.

After I see his lips stop moving, I look at Rhys to see if his reaction gives anything away, but he's just smiling stupidly, and that only makes me more curious.

Turning, I read the screen.

**The day of your accident, I told all the sporting staff I was your boyfriend so they would let me leave the field.**

His revelation leaves it wide open for me to ask the one thing that's been plaguing me since the night he kissed me. I bite the bullet and decide to ask it in front of Rhys, because if I don't ask it now, I'll chicken out.

And we're at the point where I don't think any of us has anything to hide from each other. If we did, I've been reading all of this wrong.

I swallow past the lump in my throat and go in for the kill. "Is the accident the only reason you changed your mind, or was it that you were never attracted to men before that freaked you out in the first place?"

I keep my eyes on him this time, watching the way his throat bobs as he swallows. His right hand reaches for me, and I let him twine his fingers with mine. I sneak a peek at Rhys, whose eyes dart between the two of us with nothing but concern and empathy.

Samuel's mouth opens and closes a few times before he finally talks into his phone. I'm entranced by the way his mouth moves, the frown lines in between his brows, and the way he runs his hand over his head as he contemplates which words to use that will best explain what he has to say.

He squeezes my hand and I realize he's waiting for me to read his answer. I hold on to him tightly, offering reassurance I don't think he needs but want to give him anyway.

Whatever is on that screen doesn't change a single thing in the here and now, but getting an opportunity to have insight into his thoughts is something I'll never shy away from.

I glance over to the screen and take in his words, the way I can still hear his voice as he says each and every one.

**These feelings I have for you, have always been there. Before I even considered the possibility of being bisexual, there was you. It has never felt wrong. *You* have never felt wrong.**

**But I was scared. I *am* scared. I'm always scared that I'm going to lose someone I care about. After my dad died, there isn't a single day where I don't live in fear of the next time something or somebody important to me is taken away from me.**

Tears fill my eyes and the screen blurs, the rest of the message impossible to see. I wipe my eyes as I think of how scared and confused a younger Samuel would've been. His dad, there one day and gone the next.

**As far as the accident goes, it was an epiphany of sorts. I realized
I've been holding myself back because I'm so scared to lose
someone important to me, but at least when my dad died I knew
he loved me.**

I bring his hand up to my mouth and kiss it as I raise my eyes to
meet his. Unsure if, in not so many words, he just admitted to
loving me, I don't bring attention to it. Because I don't need the
words. Deep down I've always known, and that was before I knew
what it was like to have him kiss me and touch me; before I knew
what it was like to wake up and fall asleep next to him. Before my
life was completely turned on its axis and he stuck around for all
of it.

With our hands intertwined, and his blue eyes only focusing on
mine, he tilts his head and claims my mouth.

This isn't like our first kiss.

This is clarity, certainty, and confidence.

This is *I'm yours and you are mine.*

This is *I'm sorry I took so long* and *never again.*

Slowly, we pull apart, shy smiles spreading across our faces.

Before I can put any distance between us, Samuel slides his
fingers out of mine and brings his hand that's curled into a fist, into
my line of sight.

I predict the movements before he releases his thumb, forefinger,
and pinky all at the same time.

*I love you.*

Unable to help myself, I reach out and grab a fistful of his shirt
and pull him to me, kissing him senseless.

"I love you too," I murmur against his lips. "I love you so damn
much."

Feeling on top of the world, I turn to look at Rhys, whose smile is
nothing but pride and eyes are full to the brim with happiness.

"I guess boyfriends it is."

Rhys raises his hand to his forehead and brings his thumb and forefinger together before releasing them again, as if he's holding and releasing the tip of a hat.

He then curves both his index fingers and intersects them one way and then flips them the other way. I know what he's telling me without even confidently knowing the sign. I replicate his movements, and he winks at me.

*Boyfriends.*

————

Hesitant to proceed, I'm standing in front of one of the glass conference room doors inside the UCLA library. I've been in this building countless times over the last four years, but never had I given it as much thought as I do right now.

I'm not entirely sure why I'm here. I'm not really seeking anything specific, but after advice from the audiologist, and deferring college, I realized there isn't really a lot to do with my time. I worked part time at one of the campus coffee shops, and if the broken collarbone didn't impede my serving abilities, the coffee shop isn't the best place to be navigating life with hearing loss.

I could work out with either Samuel or Rhys, or both, and now that Frankie decided to move back to LA for good, I could always hang out with him for a few hours a day too, but seriously, who wants to be everyone's tagalong?

I have a habit of keeping my circle small, choosing to live in my own comfortable, safe bubble. It's a defense mechanism I learned early on—if you speak to and trust fewer people, then there is an even smaller chance somebody could hurt you.

As much as I want to continue living like this, tightening up my world isn't going to work in my favor in these circumstances, because if I shut myself off from everything, the only one who will suffer is me.

The best way I could rationalize it in my head is comparing my circumstances to that of Arlo's and Rhys's. They are both addicts, both in recovery, and both understand that they need to have a support system in order to succeed—but their support system is made of people who have been in their shoes, who understand their troubles, who failed and who succeeded.

I need that.

I need people who have already been in my shoes, people who can reassure me that yes, there are days when it will be hard, but there are days when it will be better.

A body pushes past me, forcing me to falter on my feet. When I steady myself, I notice a girl my age, maybe a little bit younger, picking up her fallen backpack and hiking it over her shoulder. She glances up at me with green, apologetic eyes, and I salute her in greeting.

She must take this as her cue, because the next thing I know, her hands and fingers fly through a flurry of signs at a speed I'm just not used to.

With one hand, I cover both of hers, stopping her from signing and feeling guilty about it, and with my other hand, I drag my cell out of my pocket, ready to speak into it.

Her eyes dart between my hand on hers and my cell and then she nods in understanding.

It's not until this moment that I realize, I've yet to meet a person who couldn't hear me. I've spent weeks of not being able to hear anything or anybody else, but when it came to being able to vocalize my needs and wants, and have them be heard, I've had no issues.

This thought alone reiterates why professionals insist on the importance of immersing yourself into the deaf community. This exact interaction is the perfect example of the nuances surrounding being deaf and in deaf culture.

I pull up a new note on my phone and type out an introduction of sorts.

**Hi, I'm Lennox. I only lost my hearing recently and still haven't mastered the art of signing. I'm sorry I put my hand over yours.**

As she's reading, she pulls her own cell out and taps at the screen a few times before turning it to face me.

**My name is Abby. I'm sorry for assuming. And I'm so sorry for knocking into you.**

I shake my head and respond.

**Don't be, it's a shitty place to stand.**

Abby jerks her head in the direction of the conference room and then types me another message.

**Are you coming in?**

I find myself answering her eagerly, excitement blooming in my stomach.

**You know what? I think I might.**

# 21

## SAMUEL

Kisses trail back and forth across my shoulders, over and over again. I vaguely remember Lennox and Rhys leaving before I climbed into bed for a nap after my morning classes, which means I should be somewhat concerned there's someone in bed with me.

Still half asleep, I semi register the body that's draping itself on top of mine. Like me, he's wearing only briefs, and I can feel all his smooth skin gently caressing mine.

"Sammy," a familiar voice says in my ear, and a shiver runs down my spine. Rhys recently started using the same nickname Lennox gave me. It's the exact same name, but they say it differently. Lennox says it with reverence and Rhys says it with sin. "I was told to come and wake you up if you were still asleep when I got home."

He continues to pepper kisses on my shoulder and neck, and my cock stiffens against the mattress.

"I'm still asleep," I murmur into the pillow. "You should definitely keep trying to wake me up, though."

This earns me a chuckle.

"Tell me how you want me to wake you up," he says suggestively.

"Because my mind's getting away with me and I don't really want to scare you off."

I can't imagine anything he'd want to do to me being too much it would scare me away. The whole being with men thing is definitely new and different, but it also isn't a point of contention. I couldn't care less that Rhys and Lennox are men; I care about the way we treat each other. I care about the way we support one another. I care about the way being with them makes me feel and how being with me makes them feel.

I trust my body and heart to lead the way, wanting to make sure I love them right.

Yes, I love them.

With Lennox, the declaration was overdue, and with Rhys, I know it's too early. I don't want to scare him, but experience told me I'm the guy who falls first and falls hard. This doesn't seem to be any different.

"Tell me," I coax him. "Tell me all the ways you could wake me up."

"The way I could?" Sitting up, he situates himself so he's straddling me, sitting right under my ass. "Or the way I want to?"

"Want to," I breathe out. "Always want to know what you want."

He runs a single finger up and down the length of my spine. "I can't decide if I want my cock in your mouth or yours in mine."

All the blood in my body moves down to my dick. "You know, if I'm not mistaken, we can actually do both at the same time."

"We could," he says. "But I'm not going to lie, if you're going to suck my dick, I want to see your face while you do it. The way those pretty lips of yours stretch around me."

My eyes fall closed as his words sink beneath my skin, my imagination running wild.

"I wouldn't want to miss seeing just how far down your throat I could go."

He drapes his body over mine, a hand at either side of my head as he lowers his mouth to my ear. "Can you imagine it? What about me on my knees for you?" Rhys grinds on me, his erection gliding against my boxer-covered crease. "I'd open up for you, lick the length of you, suck each of your balls into my mouth."

I find myself thrusting into the mattress as my mind presses play on Rhys's words, turning them into a visual montage.

"Or maybe you'd let me get into that tight ass of yours with my tongue."

I moan just thinking about it. He nips at my ear while he tugs at my boxer briefs impatiently. Getting the hint, I raise my hips, and he drags the material over my ass and down my legs.

He wants me completely naked.

"What about this?" he croons.

His fingers ghost my crease before his hands find the globes of my ass and spend time squeezing and caressing. He then kisses me— all of me. From the nape of my neck, down to my ass, and back up again.

It's a heady feeling to be someone's focal point. He leaves me speechless when he slides his hard shaft between my cheeks.

"What about this," he repeats. "Can I have this?"

For weeks, Rhys and Lennox and I have just about kissed and licked and touched every inch of the other's bodies, and it was always enough. They could touch me less or they could touch me more, and it would always be enough.

But I'd be lying if I said I haven't thought about that next step, what it might feel like, whether or not I might like it.

"Yes," I say, clenching around him.

He rocks himself back and forth into me, and the friction to my own cock against the bedding has me desperate for more.

"You feel so good," he says. "When I'm finally inside of you, I want Lennox here so I can watch you take him in your mouth."

I feel his hot breath on my ear. "Or maybe we can take turns."

This whole song and dance is turning into an aural erotica courtesy of Rhys and his filthy mouth. His dick could've still been in his pants and I'd still be dry humping this bed like a madman.

"Before you and Lennox, sex never felt like this," he confesses as he continues to rut against me. "It was just a thing I did."

"And now?"

"And now I can't get enough." We're both rocking back and forth, mercilessly, our bodies desperate, the perfect contrast to the calm and collected tone in Rhys's voice. "Kissing, licking, sucking, any way I can have you both, I'll take it."

"We're yours," I tell him as my body tenses in anticipation of my release. "In all the ways you want us, we're yours."

"Say it again," he rasps, his control slipping. "Say it again."

The glide of his length between my ass cheeks is a tease of what it could be, and the way my cock pounds into the mattress has my balls tightening and every single muscle in my body seizing.

"I'm gonna come," I announce. "Fuck. I'm gonna come."

"Say it again," he demands, jerking into me. "I want to hear it when I come."

"We're yours," I tell him, and instantly I feel the splash of cum hit my back, like that was truly all he needed to be pushed over the edge.

"Fuck," he groans, and the sound of his bliss has me exploding all over his bed.

Rhys drapes his front over my back, his mouth at my ear, cum between us. "Say it again," he whispers.

"We're yours."

———

After cleaning up the bed and our bodies, Rhys and I, against our better judgment, return to bed. We're wrapped up in one another, my leg hiked up over his hip, his arm up and around my shoulder.

"I'm wondering how I got here with you two," Rhys says, breaking the silence. "How does a guy like me find not one, but two people who want to stick around?"

"Rhys," I growl, hating when he puts himself down. "Don't. You don't think Lennox and I feel the same? You don't think we feel lucky to have found you when the world is usually so shitty and complicated?"

I can tell by his silence that he doesn't quite grasp just how important he is to Lennox and me. I know he agrees with me, to some extent, but I'd be lying if I said I didn't notice how he's always waiting for the other shoe to drop, especially lately.

"I know I told you my dad committed suicide," I say to him, my sated afterglow giving me loose lips. "But the part that hurt the most was that nobody saw it coming."

His fingers trace patterns and lines up and down the nape of my neck as I talk.

"The day before, we were laughing and joking and he was reading to me before bed," I say before pausing, trying to swallow the emotion away. "And the next day it was all gone. And I didn't know why.

"As I got older and understood what suicide actually is and what someone like my dad was going through, it ate at me everyday that I didn't know how sad he was. He never let it show, and I was too young to read between the lines."

Leaning forward, he presses his lips gently to mine, kissing me with comfort.

"I just want to say," he starts. "The reason you didn't know your dad was struggling is because he didn't want you to know."

"I know that," I say with sadness I haven't felt in years. "But it doesn't hurt any less."

"Did you ever doubt his love for you?" he asks. "After he died?"

I shake my head. "No. I knew he loved me with everything he had. Me and my mom. There was not a single day in my life where I didn't feel his love."

"And isn't that what you said to Lennox the other day? That you were no longer scared if something bad happened, but you were more scared that you were robbing you both of the opportunity of knowing how the other felt?"

I don't know how we started the conversation with sex and then managed to move on to all things sadnesses, but I'm learning it always feels better to not have things left unsaid.

"I'm scared of anyone I care about not knowing how I feel about them." I tighten my hold on him, hoping he knows he's one of those I care about.

"I get that." His eyes veer off to the side, no longer looking at me, his gaze distant and unfocused. "It's how I feel about Kayla. Like she'll only ever know the version of me my father feeds her."

When his eyes return to me, I don't miss the longing he has for his sister.

"I'm sorry," I say.

"For what?"

"That you miss her so much."

He hikes up a shoulder. "It's not your fault."

"It's not yours either."

At this he rolls his eyes. "Were you not there the night I told you how I left her for hours unattended?"

"I heard the story loud and clear," I say. "I heard about the brother who fucked up. I heard about the brother who apologized. I heard about the brother who has a disease and is seeking help. I heard about the brother who loves his sister unconditionally." I make sure to hold his stare. "You know what I didn't hear about?" With unshed tears in his eyes, he expectantly waits for me to continue. "I didn't hear anything about a brother who needs to be the family's punching bag."

# 22
## RHYS

I've vomited no fewer than five times since I woke up this morning and it's only three o'clock in the afternoon. I can't keep anything in my stomach and nausea lodges itself in my throat every time Arlo messages me from Seattle to "check in."

The anxiety-ridden mess of a human being I am is certain he's expecting me to fuck up, while the very small sliver of rationale that tries to penetrate my thoughts reminds me that Arlo is one of my closest friends and has probably very well picked up on my mood swings all week and is more than likely just concerned about me.

I don't know what I was thinking, asking my father to meet me here. It's a place that means so much to me, and he's going to trash it to the ground. He won't see the place that saved me, the place that introduced me to Arlo and ultimately led me to Lennox and Samuel.

He won't see pride and perseverance.

He'll see nothing but another failure, and for the first time in so long, that bothers me.

"Rhys."

I continue to clean the front desk as I swallow the bile that creeps up my throat at the sound of my father's voice. I haven't seen him since the last time I told him I needed to go to rehab. When he just looked at me, with nothing but indifference on his face and said *"I suppose asking you to succeed at anything would be too much."*

I'm in a good place now; the best I've ever been. And I need to keep reminding myself of that while I'm with him.

I take a little too long to wipe the computer screen and then move on to the keyboard, and when I hear him huff, I feel a sliver of satisfaction at being able to irritate him.

It's childish and immature, but for a split second it makes me feel like I'm in control.

*One Mississippi. Two Mississippi. Three Mississippi.*

On a deep breath, I raise my head and come face-to-face with what I'll look like in another thirty years. The residual effects of my addiction meant he had size on me, more color in his cheeks, and an air of confidence I did not wear.

He could also command any space he was in, and when I was growing up, I loved it. I wanted to be just like him, but a few stints in rehab told me, I only wanted to be like him because that was the only way he would give me attention.

Over the years, I had tripped over myself and turned myself inside out to become more like him, and I failed at every turn.

"Dad," I say. "It's nice to see you."

He doesn't return the sentiment, and I try not to let it hurt.

"Is there some place we can talk?" he asks. "Somewhere a little quieter."

Nodding, I find myself changing my mind at that moment, and have him follow me to Arlo's office instead of going to sit at one of the coffee shops nearby. I don't need to wade through pointless conversation with him, he made that very clear.

When the door clicks shut, I look behind me to see my father scowling at his surroundings. I point to the couch I remember sitting on when first meeting Arlo all those weeks ago.

"Feel free to take a seat, or you could just dive right in and tell me what you want to tell me."

He rubs his hands together before putting them into the pockets of his slacks.

"We're moving," he blurts out. "Your mother and I... and Kayla. We're moving."

I find myself blinking a few times as I try to process what he's saying.

*Moving. Moving where?*

"W-what do you m-mean you're moving?" I stammer. "You mean houses? Closer to SoCal? Where are you going? Why are you going?"

He shakes his head. "Not that I need to answer you, but I got a new job and the position is based in Japan."

"You're moving *where*?" My voice trembles as I try to make sense of what he's saying. "You're moving to Japan? You're taking Kayla to Japan? I don't understand."

The air starts to feel hot and thick around me, and I find myself struggling to breathe. I use my hands to fan myself as I repeatedly circle the room.

"Jesus, Rhys, would it kill you to just sit still and listen to what I have to say," he says sternly. "We have to discuss what we're going to do with your apartment and all your expenses."

At this, I pause.

In the place where I tried to reclaim my life, my father stands here determined to be the reason I throw it all away.

I stand, frozen like a statue.

Not only is my whole family moving to Japan, but he's cutting me off, and for all intents and purposes, truly leaving me behind.

"I've got a job now," I tell him. "I've been sober for almost six months." I rattle on about all the ways my recovery is different this time, hoping to see a change in his expression. Waiting for the morsel of pride I have felt in myself lately to shift to him, so he can feel it too.

But it never comes.

He either doesn't listen or he doesn't care.

It hurts all the same.

"I could come to Japan with you," I hear myself say.

It would kill me to leave Lennox and Samuel. It might be new, but I know it's real, and that's why they'll understand. If I leave them for Kayla, they will.

A humorless laugh leaves my father's mouth. "That's not an option, Rhys. I need to sell your apartment because I'm tying up loose ends here."

He referred to me as a loose end.

Something to tie up and throw away.

Losing my balance, I fall to the floor, my knees hitting the concrete, painfully.

"Let me get this straight," I say, my voice void of emotion, almost robot-like. "You're moving to Japan, for good, with the family, and in order for you to do that you need to kick me out of my apartment." I cock my head to the side. "How soon do you need me out?"

"By the end of the month," he responds, without even an ounce of hesitation. "And I'll no longer be providing you with your monthly allowance while you look for a job."

"I just told you I found a job," I scream, completely livid at his dismissal. "I'm trying. I'm fucking trying."

He clenches his jaw. "Watch your mouth, Rhys."

Tears fueled by anger fall, my emotions having nowhere else to go but down my face.

"Can I see Kayla before you go? Please," I beg.

"For her to get attached to you only to never see you again?" He shakes his head vehemently. "That's not a good idea."

"Of course I'm going to see her again," I argue. "I'll come to Japan and see her."

"Please," he scoffs. "I will not be making her any promises you don't intend to keep."

I'm still kneeling on the ground, looking up at him like a meek, pathetic little boy, because that is all I'll ever be in front of this man. My pride, my self-worth, my dignity. My ability to love, my ability to heal. He holds all of it, bunched together like a bouquet of flowers, and he crushes them.

Over and over again.

"Get up off the floor," he says, his voice full of disgust.

When I don't move, he crouches down in front of me, and he's a man looking at a stranger. There's no love or familiarity, because he doesn't know me any more than I know him.

He's a man disappointed by his son.

And I'm a man disappointed by his father.

And that's all we'll ever be.

"We'll be in Japan indefinitely," he says. "Make it easier on yourself and pretend we don't exist. And we'll do the same. Live your life the way you want, without a care in the world for anyone else." He squeezes my shoulder. "You're really good at that."

And then he leaves.

It takes me a while to collect my thoughts and when I pick myself up off the floor, I make sure to leave all the good things I've done and acquired behind. My chest cracks at the loss and the realization, but I can't do this anymore. I can't pretend to be something I'm not.

I will never be whole. I will never be healed.

I'm just Rhys the addict. I'll never be more, and I'll always be less.

I take my cell out of my pocket and send a text before dialing a number.

A number that's seared into my brain.

A number I wish I could forget.

"Hello," the voice on the other line says. "Didn't think I would hear from you again. What do you need?"

*One Mississippi. Two Mississippi. Three Mississippi.*

"I'll take anything you got."

# 23
## LENNOX

One Mississippi. Two Mississippi. Three Mississippi.

Rhys: I'm sorry.

Samuel: What are you talking about?

Lennox: Rhys!

Samuel: Rhys!

Lennox: Where are you?

Samuel: Rhys!

# 24
## LENNOX

Rhys wasn't okay and somehow we missed it.

We'd missed it, and I don't know how Samuel and I will be able to move on from the guilt of that. We were supposed to be his comfort, his safe space, and all we'd done was let him down.

Samuel and I sit in silence in the hospital waiting room, completely flabbergasted that it's only been several weeks since my accident and here we are again.

As we wait to receive any updates on Rhys, Samuel and I struggle to have a conversation; the myriad of emotions we share, just too big to put into words. We try to put the pieces together.

What, how, why, when, and where. And every time we try, we come up blank.

But despite the lack of words, there is no physical distance between us. We can't keep our hands off each other, because Samuel's hands know what mine do.

They know how Rhys feels.

They know how he loves to be touched.

They know what it's like to hold him.

These fingers have felt the flutter of his pulse.

And his heart has beat steadily under my palm.

None of that could be forgotten.

"Are you okay?" I manage to ask Samuel.

His eyes are nothing but empty pools of blue, and it pains me to see it. The same way my heart fits both these men inside it, it breaks for both of them too. It breaks because I don't know the reason Rhys felt so alone, and it breaks a little bit more because Samuel opened up his heart to us only for his greatest fear to come true.

When I received the text from Rhys earlier, my blood ran cold at the words on the screen. His apology could've been for anything, and yet I knew exactly what it was he was apologizing for.

On instinct, I texted Frankie, needing my older brother like always. By the time it occurred to us to head to the gym, we were already too late, Frankie advising us that Arlo was Rhys's emergency contact and Rhys had already been admitted to the hospital.

It's wild how fast horrible news traveled, and yet time seems to creep on by while we wait to be allowed to see him.

Finally, Samuel nods, answering my question, and I find myself putting his comfort and fear above mine. Needing to be closer to him, I practically climb into his lap, wrap my arms around his neck, and kiss his temple. "I love you."

His hands tighten around me as he buries his head in my chest. I feel the tears on my shirt before I see them, followed by the shake of his shoulders.

I press my lips to the top of his head, whispering how much I love him, telling him again and again and again.

For Samuel, old wounds are reopening.

A ten-year-old boy, in a twenty-two-year-old man's body, processing childhood trauma through the eyes of an adult. He's breaking, right here in my arms, and I can't do anything else but act as duct tape and try to keep all the pieces of him together.

There is no way for him to think of Rhys without thinking about his father, and vice versa. The memory of one brought forth the reality of the other, and I don't know how to make any of it easier for him.

We have no details on what triggered Rhys. We don't know if it was an accidental overdose or if he was purposefully trying to end his own life. Neither answer is a comfort, but in order to know what to do next, we need to know what happened in the first place.

Eventually, Samuel raises his head, the whites of his eyes bloodshot, the blues transparent and tired. He presses his mouth to mine, the taste of his salty tears between us, and we just sit like that, in the silence.

As we're sitting, wrapped around each other, a nurse walks back to the nursing station, and Samuel pats my back, then points over to her, and I nod.

*Go see if she knows anything.*

I climb off his lap and sit on my original chair, waiting for him to return. After a short exchange, Samuel drags his phone out of his front pocket and I figure I should do the same.

His first text comes immediately.

> They're moving him out of ICU now.

> That sounds positive.

> She wouldn't give me too much information because I'm not family or his emergency contact, but she'll let me know when we can see him.

By this stage, he's taking his seat beside me, and I take the opportunity to ask him again how he's feeling.

> How are you feeling?

He pauses before answering, and I put a hand on his knee, letting him know he can take his time, I'm not going anywhere.

Samuel: I don't know.

Samuel: Nothing.

Samuel: Everything.

He glances up at me and points in my direction, asking me how I am. And the truth is, I don't know. I feel like I became more numb as time went on, because I really just have no expectations of how this is going to go once we lay eyes on him.

"I just want to be here for both of you," I tell him honestly.

Holding hands, we sit side by side and continue texting with one hand, back and forth.

Samuel: And then who's there for you?

I lean my head on his shoulder as I type.

Me: You're always here for me when I need you. You both are.

Samuel: And how are we going to be there for Rhys? What if he doesn't let us?

There is a real possibility that he won't want us to see him this way. I always knew he struggled to ask for help, and this proved me right in the worst type of way.

"We're not going anywhere." When Samuel doesn't confirm or deny my statement, I have to make sure I'm not assuming he's still in this just because I am. "Are we?"

He shakes his head.

Samuel: I don't want to lose him.

Samuel: I don't want to lose either of you.

Samuel: Ever.

He shuffles till he's on his knees in front of me, grabbing my face in his hands. He presses our foreheads together and then his mouth is on mine. He's all anger and hurt, desperation and fear, and I just want to be exactly what he needs.

I'll take it all and give him all the love back. Angry love. Hurt love. Desperate love. Scared love.

So much scared love, because that's what we are. The three of us.

Scared. So *fucking* scared.

———

"He doesn't want to see anybody else but you," I tell Arlo.

The words hurt every time I say them, but I have to constantly remind myself Rhys's needs are the most important. It doesn't matter that we just want to be there for him; I have to respect his process and hope the end goal is the same for all of us.

We were finally able to be seated in the waiting area right outside his room, but it just made it that much harder to be so close and respect his wishes to stay away.

Frankie and Arlo were in Seattle when they got the call, and it means more than I can put into words that Rhys is as important to them as he is to us. And the fact that there is at least one person he'll see now, I hope he realizes he isn't alone.

Wordlessly, Arlo nods and makes his way inside the room, and I turn to check in with Samuel as the door closes. "Are you okay?" I ask for maybe the hundredth time.

He just nods, closes his eyes, and tilts his head back.

Feeling a tap on my shoulder, I see Frankie holding his phone out to me.

**Let's go for a walk. Maybe Samuel wants a drink.**

I know if I ask he'll say he doesn't want anything, so I don't bother asking. Instead, Frankie and I head to the cafeteria, the silence with my brother the comfort that I need. It's surprisingly busy for this time of the night, and Frankie and I are standing in line when I admit something to him I never thought I would say.

"I understand why you left now."

He narrows his eyes at me in confusion, but I see his features straighten as what I'm saying registers.

"I know it wasn't exactly the same with Arlo," I acknowledge. "But that feeling when your heart drops to the bottom of your stomach…" My voice cracks, and the strength I had for Samuel is still with him in the waiting room. "And you don't know if everything is okay until you see them with your own two eyes. How many times is someone supposed to go through that?"

Not giving a single care that we're in a line, surrounded by other people, my brother turns to me, tears spilling down his face, and he collects me, and all my baggage, in his arms. We stand there for seconds or minutes, neither one of us caring or rushing.

"I'm so so sorry," I say through tears.

When we pull apart, Frankie wipes underneath my eyes and straightens my hair, the same way he did any time I was upset when we were younger.

Ordering our drinks, we take a seat in the cafeteria and Frankie slips his cell out of his jacket pocket and begins typing.

I hold my cell in anticipation.

> I should've taken you with me.

His confession stuns me

> I know that now. I should've given you the choice to come even if you would've said no.

> I would never have said no.

Now it's his turn to be stunned into silence.

> Really?

"Really," I say back. "I thought you didn't want me to come, and I made it about me, when I can see now, very clearly. It had very little to do with me at all."

> For Arlo and me, leaving hurt, but it was the best thing I ever did for his sobriety. But I will regret leaving you behind for the rest of my life.

Those tears return, but they're happy tears, grateful at the very least for the ability to be able to talk about this freely and put our regrets to rest.

> Rhys will be okay.

"How do you know?" I ask.

> Because you won't leave him. Every day you tell him he's worth it and you're happy he's here.

> Tell him you love him.

It's the one thing I haven't told him, and now I wonder if it would've made all the difference.

"I love you, Frankie," I say to my brother. "You are the only thing our parents did right by me."

# 25
## RHYS

The sound of the machines around me confirms that I am, in fact, alive. I should be relieved, and yet, the amount of shame that continues to fester on each of my organs makes me wonder if this really was the best outcome.

I feel so heavy, like every limb is filled with lead and I have to use twice the amount of effort to get them to cooperate. My brain's nothing but sludge, but just not out of action enough to forget I owe some important people some big conversations.

And for that, I'm not ready.

My whole body aches at the thought of Lennox and Samuel seeing me like this, knowing how much I've failed them, knowing how much my weakness has cost me.

They don't deserve any of this, and I hate myself that little bit more for allowing myself to become involved with them, when, with me, this was always a possibility.

"Mr. Denser." My head turns, following the voice, and I'm met with a young nurse who looks extremely apologetic for having to bother me. "We're just going to check all your vitals and then I'll get out of your hair."

After checking my temperature and my hydration levels, the nurse adjusts the pulse oximeter on my index finger and starts writing down whatever numbers the machine shows her.

"Are you feeling, okay?" she asks, interrupting my thoughts. "How about a drink of water?"

I nod, helplessly, because I really am unsure of what comes next.

"There are two men outside," she says, her voice very pleasant. "They're very eager to see you—"

I shake my head and cut her off. "No visitors."

It's cruel to have Samuel and Lennox remain on the outside, but I'm being cruel to be kind. They do not need to see me this way; they deserve better, and better is something I can't quite give.

———

I wake up for the umpteenth time, having no clue of the time of day or how much of it has passed. Noticing the sluggish feeling happens every time I open my eyes, I manage to loll my head to the side and open my eyes to slits.

I'm surprised to find Arlo sitting at the side of my bed, looking completely ruined. He takes in my appearance, and when I have nothing to say, he shakes his head and whispers, "What did you do?"

His voice is nothing but genuine concern; there's no accusation and no disappointment. He doesn't make me feel two feet tall or like a complete failure. He's just a friend worried about a friend, and this thought alone has me in a chokehold. Arlo has known me for less than two months, and with one question, he cares more for me than my own parents *ever* have.

My throat starts to close up, emotion and exhaustion getting the better of me, but I push through, these words needing to be said.

"I'm so sorry," I manage to choke out. "I'm so, so sorry."

He scoots the chair closer, and grabs my hand, nothing but empathy and heartache etched in his features. "Hey, hey. No apologies needed. We just want you to be okay."

At the mention of more than one person, my unshed tears fall and my fears and failures are the only thing I can see. "I can't let them see me like this."

My voice is pained and scratchy.

"They want to be here for you," he tells me. "We all do."

Sobs rack my body as I shake my head in complete denial. Nobody wants to be around for this.

"I did this once, too, you know," Arlo says, this bit of information taking me by complete surprise. "Lennox doesn't know. Neither does Clem or Remy. They were too young and it was too much to burden them with."

He holds my gaze. "I don't think I wanted to die," he confesses. "But I know I didn't really care about living either."

I process his revelation and ask myself some serious questions.

*Did I want to die?*

"Frankie found me," he continues. "Frankie found me and it broke his heart. He forced me to go to rehab, and I hated him for it. We wasted so much time apart because of my stupidity. Don't let it be like that with Lennox and Samuel."

I don't want to lose them, and the onslaught of panic at the thought of them pushing me away, has me wanting to rip this Band-Aid off sooner rather than later.

"Why don't I get them for you?" he offers.

Just as he stands up, my hand shoots out and grips his wrist. There's one more thing I need to tell him. He glances down at me expectantly. "It happened at work."

There are so many rules and regulations on drug use at the gym that there is no way I won't end up paying for my mistake. I hate that Arlo is between a rock and a hard place, but on some weird level, I appreciate that he has any loyalty to me at all.

"You don't need to worry about it right now," Arlo assures me. "Just focus on yourself."

*Focus on yourself.*

I don't know what that means when all I can focus on is Lennox and Samuel.

Just as Arlo reaches the hospital door, I call out to him, and he glances over his shoulder. "Do you think they'll forgive me?" I ask.

"Is there any reason they won't?"

———

They're both cautious as they step into the room, and it pains me to no end, to have them be so unsure about me. They're holding on to one another, and as always, happy or sad, they're the most beautiful whenever I see them together.

They veer out to either side of the bed, and Lennox surprises me completely when he pulls the blankets, indicating he wants to get in beside me. With the cannula in my left arm, he's able to climb in on the other side without a hitch.

Wordlessly, he shifts us until we're both on our sides and he's molded his whole body to the shape of mine. With his front to my back, he buries his head in my neck, wraps his arm around my waist, which I cover with my own, and holds me like he has no intention of letting me go.

This way, I have the perfect view of Samuel.

He pulls up the chair Arlo was just sitting on and moves it close enough that almost all of his upper body is leaning over the mattress. With my left hand resting over Lennox's, Samuel reverently places my right hand in his and brings his mouth to my knuckles, kissing every single one, then returns it gently to the bed.

His eyes fill with unshed tears, and I see just how deeply he's hurting.

I hurt them both. I hurt them differently. But I broke his fucking heart.

My left arm covers Lennox's and I squeeze it as I look at Samuel.

"I'm so sorry." The words come out on a shaky breath, and I do everything I can to hold back the tears but fail miserably when I see them streaming from Samuel's eyes.

He hides his face in the bedding, and I lift my hand to his head, playing with his hair, hopefully soothing him in the silence.

With my energy fairly depleted after the overdose, it takes little to no time for me to fall back asleep with Lennox wrapped around me and my hand buried in Samuel's hair.

When I wake again, Samuel's asleep, my hand back in his, and Lennox is still curled around me.

I feel so raw on the inside, almost too raw to talk, but there are things I need to say, things they deserve to hear.

"You're thinking too hard." Samuel's voice distracts me from my plans. He rises up off the uncomfortable chair and stretches, his shirt riding up his stomach. My eyes follow every movement, my need for him the same as it's always been. I hear him chuckle and notice he's been watching me watch him.

He bends over and kisses my forehead. "I'm going to the bathroom. Do you want me to bring you anything back? Food? Drink? Snacks?"

I reach for the collar of his shirt and tug him to me till his eyes are level with mine. "Just you. I just want you to come back."

"Always, baby." He kisses me. "Always."

When he walks out the door, Lennox sighs in my neck. "He's gorgeous, right?"

The comment is so unexpected it makes me laugh. And then I cry, holding on to Lennox when he feels my tears, because I almost gave this up. And for what?

For a piece of shit like my father?

It's at this point Samuel walks back in the room, eyeing us curiously. When he reaches the bed, I hold my hand out to him and drag him to us. I know it's almost impossible that the three of us will fit on this single bed, but Samuel understands the assignment and puts his arms over the both of us.

I grab Lennox's hand, shaping it into a fist and then rub it clock-wise over my chest.

"You don't have anything to be sorry about," he says into our makeshift cocoon. "We just want you to be okay. But if you're not okay, we still want to be around for that too."

———

I've been here for two days, and thank God I'm leaving soon. Because I'm about to rip my hair out. Samuel and Lennox have been here every waking hour, but it's been impossible to have all the important conversations and say all the important words. I've fed them dribs and drabs of where my headspace is, and they just completed my psychiatric evaluation confirming that I'm not a danger to myself or to anyone else.

It's all good news, but I just don't feel good about any of it.

A knock on the hospital door interrupts my thoughts, and when neither a doctor, a nurse, or Samuel and Lennox walk in, I look around, only to freeze when I see my mother in the doorway.

"Mom?"

"Rhys," she says, her voice as detached as ever. "I heard you were here."

"You did?"

"When your son has a reputation for engaging in a lot of drug use, you use those connections you have and make sure someone calls whenever they see him."

"I didn't know you cared so much," I say sarcastically.

She offers me a pinched smile. "I know your father visited you the other day. And told you about Japan."

*One Mississippi. Two Mississippi. Three Mississippi.*

When she doesn't elaborate, her presence begins to make me feel uncomfortable. My mother is my father's puppet. Once upon a time I believed she could've been a beautiful woman, with maternal instincts and the ability to love unconditionally and endlessly. But now...

"Is there something you came for?" I ask.

Samuel and Lennox choose this moment to walk in, and they both waste no time flanking me. Their presence calms down the rattle inside my chest.

"Kayla," she says robotically. "She's been asking about you... a lot."

"And what?"

For the first time ever, I see the slightest crack in my mother's armor as she stomps the floor and huffs. "Don't be like that, Rhys. I want you to have a relationship with her, but you know how your father is."

"Yeah," I say coldly. "I know how he is."

"Just do as I say, okay?"

I pinch the bridge of my nose. "What are you talking about?"

"Stay sober for six months."

"I'm trying, Mom," I say truthfully. "I really am."

She steps forward, and Lennox and Samuel take a few steps back to give us space. She takes hold of my face in her hands. "We had a contract. At six months you could see her, and whenever you were so close..."

Her words trail off, and my body sways enough for Samuel to steady me.

"Are you saying what I think you're saying?"

"You have a disease," she says to me, placing her hands on my shoulders and squeezing. "And he used it to his advantage."

"What?" My body shakes in shock as I find myself near the edge of the bed and I sit. "Mom, please tell me what to do."

"We'll start small," she says. "Letters, FaceTime, texts. And when you're both ready, you can visit us in Japan."

She looks around at Samuel and Lennox. "You can even bring your friends, as long as you're there."

"But, Rhys..." I nod. "Six months. No less."

Unlike with my father, this isn't a threat. The words leaving her mouth are like a plea. A revelation. A lifeline I never saw coming.

"It's good to see you all," she says, her manners impeccable as always. "Rhys." She straightens her spine. "I hope to see you in six months' time."

# 26
## RHYS

A few more hours after my mother's surprise visit and I'm finally being discharged. I've been on autopilot for the whole afternoon, trying to process it all, and coming up empty.

Her revelation changed everything and nothing.

Maybe I've been looking for solace in the darkness, to fill the empty void that being an unloved son gave me, but I understand free will and know that that man didn't put a gun to my head and force me to abuse drugs.

But the confirmation that he truly does feel absolutely nothing for me at all, stings more than it has any right to. Especially when the writing was on the wall—it wasn't a surprise. In fact, he constantly went out of his way to belittle me and remind me that I'm absolutely nothing without him and his money.

Samuel and Lennox have been wearing kid gloves around me, more so after my mother bombarded us at the hospital, but now, as we're on our way home, I don't want any special consideration between us. I want to strip us all bare and lay our secrets down once and for all.

Especially mine.

It takes us about half an hour to get back to my place, and when they follow me through the door, it's like we're all strangers, and I hate it.

Standing in the middle of the apartment, I drop my small duffle bag to the floor, and Samuel's head is the first to turn, then Lennox follows his lead.

The three of us are staring at each other, the air layered with thick and heavy emotion.

The walls of the hospital wrapped around us like a bubble, but here, at my place, where we made some of the best memories, the three of us are naked and vulnerable with absolutely nowhere to hide.

They have seen me at my lowest, and even I can't stomach to look at myself in the mirror, let alone expect someone else to.

"I can see your thoughts ticking over," Lennox says softly. Almost like he's scared that just one wrong word will disrupt the quiet. "But you're wrong. Nothing is different," he says, picking up on every one of my insecurities. "You are the same. *We* are the same."

My lip does an involuntary quiver and I bite on it to stop myself from crying, because he's wrong, *everything* is different now.

If they don't want to move forward, I'm not sure how I'll ever go back, because a life without them isn't an option for me.

When I don't say anything, Lennox closes the distance between us, each step nice and slow. He holds his hand out for me to take, and when I do, he surprises me by guiding me into the bathroom.

He stops us right in front of the mirror, and when I look at my reflection, I can see both Lennox behind me and Samuel leaning comfortably against the doorjamb.

He reaches for the hem of my shirt and drags it up my body. I take in my appearance and notice, despite my hospital stay, I've been regaining a lot of the weight and shape I'd lost over the years.

Lennox's mouth starts at one exposed shoulder and moves its way across to the other.

He does it again and again, almost like a distraction, before hooking his fingers inside my waistband and pushing my sweats and boxers down my legs.

"Is this what you need?" he asks as he drops open mouthed kisses all over my skin.

My cock thickens as I watch us through the reflection.

"Do you need me to kiss every inch of you?" *Kiss. Kiss. Kiss.* "Do you need me to kiss every inch of you so you know there's not a single thing on this damn earth that changes what we have?" The intensity of his words is a delicious contrast to the lightness of his touch. "Because I'll do it."

I groan, my head falling back against Lennox's shoulder, and he wraps a hand around my length.

The sound of running water has me acknowledging Samuel's presence, and shivers race down my spine when I feel his hand join Lennox's.

"He's actually wrong," Samuel says softly. "Things *have* changed. Now we just want you more."

I don't let him say anything more, the sentiment enough to have me slamming my mouth to his. God, how I missed this. The kiss feels like a jolt of electricity has just been shot through me. Like a live wire, surging through my veins, reminding me that I'm alive.

I try to kiss him back with as much ferocity, but he completely devours me. His mouth bruising, his tongue owning mine. While Lennox's touch is nowhere to be found.

Because he can always read my mind, Lennox's voice is in my ear. "You keep kissing him," he orders. "Don't do anything else."

Lennox loves his control, and usually I love finding ways to make him give it up, but right now I will do everything his mouth tells me to do. I want to be under his thumb. I don't want to think. I don't want to move. I don't want to breathe unless he tells me to.

Reluctantly, Samuel pulls his mouth off mine, and I manage to pry my eyes open to see the reason why. Lennox whispers something in Samuel's ear, and their gazes find mine. He gives Lennox a quick nod, and my pulse flutters beneath my skin in anticipation.

Samuel quickly removes his clothes and pulls me inside the shower with him, and I gladly stand under the steady stream, letting the hot water wash away all the grime and dirt of my hospital stay. As if he's had the same thought, he squirts body wash on his hands and lathers up my skin.

When he turns me to face him, my eyes don't miss the opportunity to dance around the wonder that is his body. His thick thighs, his heavy cock, his rigid chest.

His touch is soft and soothing, and there is no rush or race to whatever comes next. His mouth finds mine, and this kiss is a complete contrast to the fire that was lit between us earlier.

The shower is small on the best of days, but as Lennox's naked body presses up behind me, I'm suddenly grateful for the unaccommodating space, because I need to get out of my own head, and these two know it.

There isn't a single inch of me that isn't surrounded by them touching me, kissing me, teasing me. When they both drop to their knees on either side of me, I'm sure I died in that hospital and went to heaven.

There is no doubt they had this planned, Samuel wrapping his wet lips around my cock while Lennox spreads my ass cheeks and chooses this moment to feast on my hole.

I can't move.

I can't think.

I can't breathe.

It's everything I need this moment to be.

I watch Samuel's cheeks hollow out as his mouth moves up and down, sucking me greedily. Hungrily.

"Fuck, Sammy baby, I'm going to come."

Lennox's finger surprises me, slipping between my crease and breaching my hole. "You're close, aren't you?" he taunts, finding my prostate. "Come, baby. Come in his mouth," he coaxes. "I want to see it spilling out from the sides so I can lick it all up."

I moan at the visual and my whole body strains like a slingshot ready for release.

Lennox shifts me so my back hits the wall, and all I can see is him and Samuel on their knees, both in line with my cock. Together, they devour my aching length, licking and sucking and kissing each other in between.

All tongues and mouths, my orgasm barrels out of me at the sight of them worshiping me like I'm a god, on their knees, fighting over my cock. My chest almost collapses at the lack of air getting into my lungs as my body trembles with the enormity of my release.

No, I'm definitely not a god.

But I'm irrevocably *theirs*.

———

If I doubted whether or not these men were made for me, the way they could read my every need without me uttering a single word was proof enough.

The edge has been taken off and I'm now out of my head enough to know that we have things to talk about, but whether or not these two men are mine and want to remain so, isn't it.

The three of us are dry and naked, under the bedding, limbs tangled until you can't tell whose leg or arm is whose. Lennox is in his favorite place, behind me, and Samuel is tracing the lines on my face with his fingertips, as if committing them to memory, just in case.

Just like at the hospital, I grab Lennox's hand and have him sign the word *sorry* over my chest.

"I know you're sorry," he says. "But I don't think either of us are looking for an apology."

Sighing, I turn out of his hold and sit up, looking for my cell. I don't want to sugarcoat it for them, but more than that, I don't want them to sugarcoat it for me.

I see the pain in their eyes, I recognize their hurt, and I want them to know that my recovery will always depend on knowing the consequences of my actions.

*All* the consequences, not just the dangerous ones.

When I see my cell on the nightstand, I stretch over Samuel and grab it. I want to do this right. I want to be as effective in my communication as possible, and I want Lennox to know how much I mean everything I've been feeling.

I sit upright, my lap covered, open my notes app, and begin typing. It takes a while, and Samuel and Lennox just lie there, their arms around my waist, their heads burrowed in my lap. It's obvious none of us are currently seeking personal space.

After typing for a good ten minutes, I ruffle Lennox's hair and hand him the phone.

"What's this?" he asks as both he and Samuel sit up with me.

I point to the top of the screen where I've written the instructions. Lennox's eyes dance across the words, and I have to put my hand over the screen to stop him. I run my fingers up and down his arm. *Slow.*

He touches his thumb to his chest, his hand spread out like the number five. *Fine.*

"My first mistake was not telling you both about my father reaching out to me," he reads. "I don't want to be a burden to anyone."

At this, Samuel sits up and drags me between his legs, folding his arms around me.

"You're not a burden," he whispers before kissing me on the temple.

Lennox continues to read to us what I wrote. "I know this isn't true, but I always feel like the least put together person in any group setting. That feeling has carried me through almost every relationship I've ever had. It's the main reason why I try to deal with things on my own."

Lennox's lips purse, and I know he's storing up all his rebuttals for every single observation about myself I listed, and I'm looking forward to it.

I'm looking forward to the honesty between us and the weight to lift.

Lennox slides his hands into mine as he keeps reading.

"When they did the psychiatric evaluation at the hospital, it stated that I wasn't a danger to myself." His throat bobs. "But I truly don't know what outcome I would've preferred that night."

Swallowing hard, he looks up at Samuel and me. "And that's what scares me the most."

## 27
### SAMUEL

Even hearing the words out of Lennox's mouth doesn't dampen just how much they hurt to hear. Everything else Rhys admitted didn't faze me.

We're all human and we're all imperfect. It isn't the first or the last time that we would assume we didn't need somebody's help, or we're worried that we might be too much of a burden.

These things I can handle.

I can't handle that he doesn't know if it was an accidental overdose or not. I know it isn't fair to put my fears and expectations on him while he's in recovery and it's all still so fresh, but his uncertainty is my biggest fear.

I do not want to live in a world that is too hard for him to live in.

I don't want to live without him or Lennox. At any point. And maybe that's the issue at hand. I haven't been explicit in my feelings for him, and I need to be.

"You can't die," I blurt out. "If you feel like you don't want to be here, promise me you'll talk about it."

My eyes meet Lennox's and a pang of guilt hits me, but he puts his hand up before I'm able to say anything.

"Intention is everything," he says. "Your intention is to not leave me out of the conversation, it always has been. And truth be told, sometimes conversations aren't about me and they don't include me. It's going to happen. But, please, don't stop yourself from telling him how you feel because of me."

I mouth *"I love you,"* something we've been practicing, and he smiles and says, "I know."

Shifting, I move myself underneath the blanket so Rhys and I are face-to-face.

"You can't die," I repeat. "You can't die without talking to me. You have to let me at least try and help first."

It's so morbid to talk about suicide like it's inevitable, but I don't believe in leaving things unsaid, not anymore, not after my father's death, and not after what happened with Rhys.

I grab his face with my hand. "It's the only promise I'll ever ask you to make," I tell him. "Promise me."

"I promise," he says with a shaky breath. "I promise to always talk to you." He offers Lennox a sad smile. "I'll talk to you both if and when I need to. I promise."

It's a simple request, yet it holds such stigma and weight, and I want to make sure Rhys knows this is not up for discussion. It isn't for either of them. But Lennox has been told time and time again, and if I have to repeat it one hundred more times to the both of them, I will.

"Good." I bring his forehead to mine. "Because I'm in love with you, and I like to keep what I love."

"I don't think anybody has ever loved me before," he says softly. "Besides Kayla, I don't think I've loved anyone else either."

The small admission lands perfectly on my heart as I watch Lennox come up from behind Rhys, wrap an arm around his neck, and kiss him on the cheek. "We're not going anywhere. No matter what happens and no matter how bad it hurts. Nothing you do or say or feel is going to scare us away."

Rhys turns his face enough for Lennox to capture his mouth in the sweetest kiss. When they part, Lennox whispers, "I love you."

Rhys looks between us and then holds his hand out for me, tugging me closer.

Cupping the back of my head, he brings my mouth to his, and clearly does the same to Lennox.

Our lips move as our bodies rut and roll against one another. We're all tongues, teeth, hands, and legs as I try to climb under their skin and they try to climb under mine.

Lennox's finger ghosts the crease of my ass as Rhys and I grind our cocks together.

"I want inside you," Lennox whispers. "While you're inside Rhys."

Rhys and I both moan at the visual, increasing the friction between us.

"Don't blow it yet, I'll be back to slick you both up."

He slaps my ass as he leaves, and Rhys and I continue rutting and kissing, a sense of relief pouring over me for the first time in days.

He's home. He's safe. He's mine.

"I love you," he says in between kisses. "I love you. I love you. I love you."

The bed dips upon Lennox's return, and he hovers over us, hands and fingers all slicked up, commanding our bodies every which way.

When Rhys is on his back, legs spread open, I glide my cock over his hole, over and over again, sliding and inching the tip inside of him.

"Fuck, you feel good," I say as I tease us both, going a little bit deeper each time.

At the same time, Lennox chooses to torture me, using only his fingers, testing my concentration as he slides his slick fingers up and down my taint.

"Fuck him," he orders. "I want to see if I can drive you both crazy."

The Lennox behind closed doors is the complete opposite to the man he is with everyone else. He commands and dominates; he makes sure he's steering our ship and Rhys and I just follow.

Hovering over Rhys, I finally push all the way inside of him, loving how his moan echoes around the room. As I find my rhythm, Lennox fills my ass with three thick fingers, stretching me wide as I try to concentrate and distinguish between both sensations.

Rhys's arms circle my neck, dragging me down to kiss him.

We're all teeth and tongues as my hips begin to rock into him persistently, loving the contrast of my cock inside Rhys and Lennox's fingers inside me.

Just as I'm getting used to the full feeling, Lennox drags his fingers out and I whimper from the loss. My own cock slipping out of Rhys.

"Fuck," I groan.

Holding my length, I line it up with Rhys, just as I feel Lennox line the head of his cock up with my hole. I know Lennox, I know he's either going to push it in slowly or sync it up to be the exact moment that I push inside of Rhys.

But even knowing the two possibilities, I'm unprepared for the way my body pistons into Rhys's body as Lennox slams into mine.

Our voices bounce off the walls as the sound of skin slapping skin creates an erotic symphony. The three of us in perfect synchronicity.

And it's not just sex.

It's the way we feed off each other, the way we bleed for each other.

It's the perfection from the very beginning of seeing someone for the very first time and not needing any reason or any rhyme to know in the marrow of your bones that they were made for you.

It's the heartache.

It's the tragedy.

It's the downfall.

Mine is theirs and theirs is mine.

I reach around and squeeze Lennox's leg, letting him know I'm too close to crawl my way back.

And then I grab Rhys's cock and stroke it furiously.

"Come, baby. Let go and come for me."

# 28

## LENNOX

### FOUR WEEKS LATER

"Goodbye, Mom. Goodbye, Dad," I call out to Rhys and Samuel, who feel the need to drop me off to my support group themselves every other week.

Abby is waiting for me as I walk toward the library entrance, her phone in hand. I bring my cell phone to my face, knowing she's about to send me a text in three...two...one.

> Really, Lennox, you got yourself two boyfriends?
>
> It's so unbecoming of you to be so greedy.
>
> What about the rest of us?

After the first time we met, Abby and I became inseparable. She reminds me of Clem with her feisty attitude, except she has a softness about her that makes me feel like the older sibling this time around.

I didn't know you were in the market for two boyfriends. The other day you could barely handle that guy at the coffee shop flirting with you.

Please. Be for real. I can't exchange texts with a guy who doesn't use full sentences and punctuation. Don't come at me with acronyms, because nine out of ten times I'm going to get them wrong, on purpose, and then we're all screwed.

K

You're a dick.

No, I have a dick.

Same-same if you ask me.

We're making our way through the automatic doors, when another text comes through.

So, I was thinking. Do you want to come see this indie band with me this weekend?

Sorry, I told you I was taken, but thank you.

*eye roll emoji*

Please scroll up to see the aforementioned insult.

You can bring them.

Abby has been slowly becoming my go-to person whenever I have any questions, concerns, or doubts; she walks and talks me through it all. The best thing about our friendship is that being deaf is the least interesting thing about the both of us.

She's currently studying to get her bachelor's degree in cyberse-curity, and to be honest, it's no surprise the guy from the coffee shop didn't meet her standards. I'm surprised she can even handle having a conversation with me; she's out of everyone's league.

> Text me the details. And I'll let you know if we can make it.

The support group we attend is for college students who are Hard of Hearing and/or Deaf people. Despite no longer being enrolled in college, my deferment and doctor's diagnosis were used as proof that I could use the school's service till my eventual graduation.

Besides meeting Abby, the group is currently allowing me to explore all the ways UCLA makes their classes, content, and campus accessible to deaf students.

It continues to blow my mind just how little time I spent thinking about anything outside my world. I thought being a foster kid made me less privileged and more understanding, because I somehow knew what struggle really meant. But between my recent diagnosis and life with Lennox and Samuel, my perception of the world has been changing.

Some for the worse.

Some for the better.

Along with the support group, I've finally enrolled in a face-to-face sign language class, and so have Samuel, Frankie, Arlo, Clem, and Remy. It's a little bit ridiculous that we all insisted on going to the same class, and all together, but they're being supportive, and I'd be lying if I said I don't love it.

After class we usually all spend time annoying the shit out of Rhys by practicing our signs. We all know a lot of signs but lack the speed to have a back-and-forth conversation. But with Rhys we practice incorrectly, on purpose. Just so he can show us the right way.

One of my favorite things to do is see him and Samuel interact with my family. It brings me a sense of contentment I didn't realize I've spent my whole life searching for.

I know I'm only twenty-two, but the one thing foster care did teach me was the difference between a house and a home. I've lived in a lot of houses.

Came and went. Hated and loved.

But Samuel and Rhys? They are unequivocally my home. I've never felt more settled, more supported, and more me than I do with them.

Sometimes I think I may have lost my hearing, but I gained them, and there is no sound in the world that I need more than I need them.

When my phone vibrates, I expect it to be Abby giving me shit for my wayward thoughts, but it's Clem.

> What are you doing this afternoon?

> I don't have any concrete plans but Rhys and Lennox will be picking me up from the library soon. Why? Is everything okay?

> I'm getting my hair done, and I want you to see it.

> Can I not see it when you get home?

> But where's the fun in that?

There's something going on with her, but I know better than to pry. Clem is the type of person who shares her secrets if you ask; she just never offers them out of her own free will.

I text her back.

> Where is this hair salon anyway? Because I'm at UCLA this afternoon.

She pin drops me the location and I see it's in walking distance from the library. I open up my message thread with Samuel and let him know where to pick me up.

> Abby and I will be here after we're done at the library.

I attach the location and wait for his response.

> You didn't look like you needed a haircut the last time I saw you.

> How funny. I'm meeting up with Clem.

> Okay, that makes more sense. I'll see you soon.

When Abby and I finish up with our group, she agrees to come with me to meet Clem at the salon.

> So let me get this right, Clem is your foster sister?

> Yes, I have one biological brother and three foster siblings. Two boys and one girl.

By nature Abby is very inquisitive, and I find I never have any issues telling her what's going on in my life. After Rhys's accidental overdose, she became someone I could depend on for sound and logical advice.

As soon as we arrive at the salon, I take in the nice, swanky place, surprised that Clem is even here. She's usually a color-in-a-box-from-the-store type of girl. I notice her in one of the chairs, the stylist blow drying her now dark-red hair.

She looks as gorgeous as ever but different, older and more mature.

I let Abby know which one Clem is and type out a text to let her know I'm here.

> Your hair is definitely worth the trip over.

She smiles as she reads it and then glances around the place to find me. When she spots me, she waves and then says something to her stylist. They finish up her hair, and both of them walk toward us.

"I never imagined you as a redhead," I tell her when she reaches me. "But now I can't see you as anything else."

She proudly shakes her head from side to side and then splays her right hand against her chest before pulling it away and making her middle finger and thumb come together, signing the word "like."

"I love it," I answer. My eyes dart to the stylist, who is just staring at Clem with stars in her eyes, and suddenly I'm heavily transfixed on their exchange. The woman is older, skin a little darker, hair brown but bordering along black.

She leans forward and tucks some of Clem's hair behind her ear before kissing her on the cheek. When I turn to Abby, she pretends to fan herself and we both laugh, gaining Clem's attention.

"Sorry," she signs, and I shake my head. We aren't in a rush.

When she finishes up, I don't miss the kiss the stylist plants on Clem's cheek or how red they turn at the gesture. Pretending I didn't see anything, I lead Abby to the front of the shop only to be met with Samuel, leaning against his car and looking like a snack I just want to devour.

Jumping into his embrace, my mouth finds his for a quick kiss.

"Where's Rhys?"

He signs the letter G and rotates his wrist. *Gym.*

"Are we picking him up?"

At this he grabs his phone and just continues the conversation in text.

> Samuel: We're all meeting at Cali Burgers.
> Apparently, Arlo and Frankie have news.

I already know what the news is, but I'm excited to see how everyone reacts when Frankie and Arlo share it.

By the time we're all packed into Cali Burgers, Remy and Abby are in a deep conversation about computer firewalls and Frankie is obsessing over Clem's new hairstyle.

Samuel wraps his arms around me and his breath ghosts over my ear. *I love you.*

He follows it up with our favorite sign, but I don't need it to know when he says it, he's feeling it.

It's everywhere and in everything.

It's as permanent as my pulse, beating every second of every day.

He leans in for another kiss, and when we part, I see Arlo and Rhys walking into the diner together. Still looking apprehensive, it has taken Rhys a moment to not worry about whether anybody judges him over his relapse.

Even though everybody has gone out of their way to ensure he knows he is the priority in our lives, I know accepting what we say is the truth can only happen in his time.

When his eyes land on Samuel and me, his face splits into the smile he only ever reserves for us. He moves to grab a seat but Samuel tugs on his hand and drags him into his lap, ensuring he's closer to us. Always reminding him, in any way he can, *we want you here.*

When seated, Rhys buries his head in my neck. *I love you.*

This time I'm the one who follows it up with the sign, making sure Rhys feels it, making sure he knows that my love for him is unconditional.

That my love for him is everywhere and in everything.

It's as permanent as *his* pulse, beating every second of every day.

The three of us love differently. The way we show love and the way we receive it. But it's the presence of love in its entirety that makes any of this possible at all.

# 29
## SAMUEL
### SIX WEEKS LATER

"Happy Birthday."

My mom's face fills up the computer screen, her smile contagious.

"Thank you, Samuel honey. It's so good seeing you. How are you?"

My mom and I talk all the time. We're close, in a Gen Z type of way. We text. A lot. But phone calls and FaceTimes are saved for special occasions. Like her birthday.

"I'm good, Mom. How are you?"

"It's the same old thing over here," she says flippantly. "Just another year older, you know that. And how are those beautiful boys of yours?"

Those beautiful boys of mine are still tangled up in bed together, but I figure she doesn't need to know all the details about our life together.

It's so funny to me how much she loved them in such a short amount of time, and yet it isn't surprising at all. My mother is a woman with a lot of love to give. Even growing up with my friends from school, she was always a safe space.

The mother you could tell your secrets to and she would still manage to console or reprimand you while making you feel like you were heard and understood.

I'm so lucky to have her.

And it's another reason as to why when I finally found the time to tell her about Lennox and Rhys, it was probably the most anticlimactic conversation she and I have had to date. I didn't anticipate any one single reaction, but I expected some questions, or at least some poking and prodding. Some curiosity when I mentioned that not only am I bisexual, but more importantly I'm part of a throuple.

She's the one who uses that word. I couldn't give a shit about any of that stuff, but she thinks she's hilarious for it, while I just continue to bask in the love of a mother, I *know* not everyone receives.

After my dad died, we kind of fell into this understanding where you didn't leave any stone unturned when it came to the ones you loved. You didn't make decisions based on assumptions and you always asked for clarification when needed.

People find it annoying.

People often push you away.

But later on, you learn that the same people really just want you to stay, want you to care, want you to love them, they just don't know how to ask.

I learned this all from my mother, and it's the reason after Rhys's overdose, she's the only person who understands exactly what I'm feeling.

The hurt.

The confusion.

The *fear*.

I tried not to let it show, but for the first few weeks I was scared all the time. Scared that there was such a fine line between relapse and suicide. Scared that one mistake could have such grave consequences. I was scared to lose him, period.

But there was my mother, reminding me constantly about the things I should and could be changing. She reminded me every day to normalize conversations between men about their feelings. She reminded me every day to normalize conversations between *my* men.

*My* men.

I absolutely love it when she calls them that, because that's what they are; they're mine. And I want to protect and love and cherish what's mine any way I can.

Rhys's overdose brought up both a lot of old and many new feelings for me. There was so much unresolved trauma that I didn't even know existed, but the truth is, it's hard to know if you've processed something as enormous as suicide at the age of ten.

I mean, I knew my father was dead.

He was gone and not coming back.

Those concepts as a ten-year-old are hard to understand but not impossible. What's impossible is trying to explain to your ten-year-old son that suicide is not a reflection on how much you loved your loved one.

Like Rhys himself had told me once, my father's love for me and my love for him had nothing to do with why he took his own life. Those things weren't at all mutually exclusive, and that's what made it all so much more difficult to process.

It was such a nuanced topic and my thoughts were black and white. They were sometimes too  innocent and childlike, because I knew the difference, and I knew reality. I just didn't ever want to have to deal with the truth.

"And what's got you thinking so hard over there?" my mother asks me, reading me like a book.

"Nothing," I assure her. "Nothing that can't wait till it's not your birthday."

She offers me a sad, yet beautiful, smile as her doorbell rings. Her face scrunches up, looking so put out.

"Are you going to answer it?" I ask her.

She shakes her head. "No, if it's a package, they can just leave it at the door."

Of course this is her response.

"Mom," I say through a tight smile. "Please go and see what it is."

It takes a handful of seconds for her to understand, and her eyes light in excitement. With her back to her laptop screen, I quickly send a message to Lennox and Rhys.

> Me: It's time. Hurry up and get your asses out here. I'll blow you both later.

It takes less than twenty seconds for them to appear in the kitchen, both of them trying to put clothes on in record time.

I watch her open her apartment door, and I can hear the squeal she makes when she sees what's on the other side. Now Rhys and Lennox are on either side of me as she comes back into view. She puts the cake beside her.

"Oh my goodness. What a beautiful surprise it is to see you both this morning." She glances at Lennox and then knocks a fist on the table. "Fuck."

She then signs "sorry."

I can't help but laugh because I know we all interpreted her curse word just fine.

"It's fine, Mom," I reassure her, knowing she's been very mindful to start learning sign language for Lennox.

Like I said, she's that type of mom.

"Don't worry, Ms. Hart," Lennox says. "These two can let me know what's going on. Now, let's see what's in that box."

His words ease her anxiety as she opens up the cake box. She turns it to ensure we can see what she does and then unshed tears fill her eyes.

My mother is also a crier.

"Put the candles in," I instruct, "and then light them up."

She follows my instructions, and as soon as the flames come into view, the three of us burst into song and sing her a very out of tune "Happy Birthday."

Both Lennox and Rhys lean into me, and I wrap an arm around

each of their waists in gratitude, as we watch my mom blow out her candles.

Here in these four walls, everybody I care about is within my reach.

Life, happiness, love, they're all here, within my reach, and mine for the taking. And I *am* going to take it. All of it, with these two men by my side and my mother reminding all of us that there is nothing wrong with those of us who feel too much or feel too little.

There is no happy medium.

There is just happy.

Find it.

Be it.

And with them, I can.

With them, I will.

Find it.

Be it.

Happy.

Rhys, Lennox, and my mother continue talking for a few minutes longer, until Mom says she's going to get going and cut up some slices of cake for her neighbors. We say our goodbyes and make plans for when she can finally meet *my* men in person.

When her face disappears off the screen, Lennox slams the laptop closed. "We were promised a blow job, and I don't need technology to fail us and your mother see us shove two dicks down her precious son's throat."

Nodding, Rhys smirks and grabs his cock.

I bring my hand to rest just under my chin and flick my fingers out, signing the word *filthy*.

Lennox licks his lips and winks at me. "Just how you like me."

# 30
## RHYS
### EIGHT WEEKS LATER

"Hi," I choke out. "My name is Rhys Denser and I've been sober for fifty-six days."

I hadn't known that Arlo and Frankie would be here when I decided I wanted to speak at this meeting, or when I asked Lennox and Samuel to join me.

I told them they didn't have to come, but whenever I said the words "I want," Lennox and Samuel made it their life mission to make sure "I got"

But I'm finally in a good enough place to get myself back into the program and reconnect with Jenika. It brings about as much shame to me as it does hope, and I'm getting used to every good feeling I have, having a dark side that I feel even harder.

But I'm learning to lean into the positive. To look for it in the little things and celebrate those little things. I'm learning to be grateful for the supportive people I have in my life, for the people who are there every step of the way, catching me when I fall, supporting me when I try to get back up.

My life is important. I need to remember that, and I need others to remind me of it. Prioritizing myself isn't weak, and setting bound-aries isn't an imposition.

No is no, and enough is enough.

So much has happened in such a short space of time, but it finally feels like the world has slowed down a smidgen and is allowing me to join in on the ride.

I glance around the room, noticing Lennox and Samuel at the back. They have organized an ASL interpreter and I'm grateful that some, if not all, of what I say will be understood by Lennox.

"Hi," I repeat. "My name is Rhys Denser and I've been sober for fifty-six days. I couldn't tell you at what age I started taking drugs. I know there was a teen at the end of a number, and whatever number it was, it was way too early. Like most teens, I partied and I partied hard. I also had parents who had busy lives and a lot of money. All in all, I got what I wanted, when I wanted it."

Feeling my body shake with anxiety and nervousness, I focus on the two men at the back of the room who refuse to let their gazes drop from mine.

My rock.

My anchor.

"Once I was partying regularly, the drugs flowed and I was particularly partial to the way they made me feel. If my parents were bothered that I was never home and always high, they didn't say a word. But if my parents were at home and I was bothering them, that was another story.

"As I got bolder and more out of control, their grip started to tighten, and my father and I continued in this game of cat and mouse, him making rules and me breaking them. I then also started to learn that I liked being the lazy, incompetent son that he so often described, because nobody expected anything of him, and soon enough I was drowning in a drug addiction, because I had too much time on my hands and a point to prove to my father.

"This was my life and I was going to live it anyway I wanted to."

I clear my throat as I reflect on the time in my life when it all took a turn. The day I changed my life and my sister's, and everything else that followed.

"My name is Rhys Denser, and I have been sober for fifty-six days." I repeat it again to remind myself that it is the good part of the story. As I rehash all the bad and the ugly, I continue to remind myself that I am Rhys Denser and I have been sober for fifty-six days, and good things do happen.

"I have friends, I have a job." I smile at Rhys and Lennox before the words leave my mouth. "I am embarrassingly in love, and I am determined to, one day soon, see my sister. I am Rhys Denser, and I have been sober for fifty-six days.

"Sometimes we don't know where our story starts, or what the triggering moment was to kick off our addictions. Sometimes it's nothing, and sometimes it's everything. Sometimes we're a mess of broken hearts and bones, and sometimes we're raised to be solid soldiers and we so desperately want to feel."

I feel my body straighten as a sense of peace settles over me.

"I am also Rhys Denser who has been useless, forgetful, and hopeless. I have been unloveable and disappointing. I have relapsed multiple times and have been all the names my father used to dismiss and demean me. The truth is, I can be both people, the one I'm learning to love and the one I hate, and still want more. Still. Deserve. More.

"My name is Rhys Denser and I've been sober for fifty-six days."

————

"Can I talk to you for a minute?" Jenika's voice interrupts my conversation with another person from the group.

"I'll be right back," I murmur, offering them a small smile and then turning to see her.

"It's really good to see you," she says. "I had a feeling you might've been avoiding me."

"I was," I say truthfully.

After finding out that the gym was Jenika's, and knowing I broke the cardinal rule about drugs on the premises, I was filled with an unrivaled amount of shame and embarrassment.

It's one thing to fuck up when your father is nothing more than a rich prick, but it's another to trash the life's work of someone you've grown to respect and care about.

"I didn't know how to make amends."

"You work at the gym for free, Rhys." She tilts her head. "That seems like some kind of amends to me."

"It's not free," I argue. "You pay me."

"Peanuts," she says. "I pay you peanuts."

I hike my shoulders up to my ears and hold my hands out. "It is what it is."

"I've been keeping tabs on you through Arlo."

I cock an eyebrow at her.

"I know, it's not very professional," she says, chastising herself. "But I was worried about you. And he didn't breach your confidence, just told me things on a need-to-know basis about my employees."

A chuckle rumbles in my throat. "Seems very professional."

If there's one thing my relapse has taught me, it's that a lot more people give a shit about you than you think. In those moments you always feel so alone. So helpless and assume not a single soul can help you.

Turns out, if you ask, you will find someone.

My head swivels around the room, searching for Lennox and Samuel, only to find they're already looking my way. When I met them, all I could see was the way they fit with one another, the seamless way they read each other's thoughts and fulfilled each other's needs. How beautiful they looked with each other, how much love and respect surrounded their relationship.

I think they're perfect for one another, and it is as easy as breathing loving both men, but it's what it feels like to be loved by them that is the real treasure. I am loved unconditionally. I am loved more for every flaw I have. I am loved for my mistakes, and I am loved for my mishaps. I am loved for my sins and my scars.

They love me and all my imperfections.

For some, it's till death do us part.

For others, it's through sickness and health

For us, it is to hell and back.

I feel Jenika's eyes on mine as the three of us get lost in a trance of each other. I chew on the corner of my bottom lip and raise a closed fist and release my thumb, forefinger and pinky all at the same time.

*I love you.*

Jenika reaches for my forearm, bringing my gaze back to hers. "Truly, Rhys. How are you?"

I can't help but look back at them. "I'm happy. I'm really, really happy."

# ONE MISSISSIPPI
## LENNOX: EIGHT YEARS OLD

I place my hand on my knee to stop it from bouncing and try to will away the ugly feeling inside my stomach.

"It's going to be a good day," I murmur to myself. "It's going to be a good day."

"Lennox, are you ready?"

My social worker, Grace, stands in front of me, smiling and holding out her hand. Usually, her presence alone calms me down, but today it doesn't work.

"It's going to be a good day," I repeat under my breath. "It's going to be a good day."

"What's that?" she asks, assuming I'm talking to her.

"Nothing," I mumble.

"Are you excited?"

*Excited.*

I know the word. I know what it means. But I don't think I've ever felt true excitement in my life. In fact, I'm certain I don't know what excitement feels like.

Sadness.

Pain.

Fear.

I know how those things feel, and I feel them often. But excitement? That isn't a real thing. Just like happiness and smiling. Those are things I heard other kids talk about. Saw other kids do.

Not me.

Not Lennox York.

"Your brother is excited to see you," she adds. *Is excited the only word she knows?* "I think you're going to love living with him."

I want to laugh, even though I didn't find anything Grace said funny. Yes, she's kind and patient and always had tissues and candy on hand when she came for visits, but she's also a liar.

All adults are.

This isn't a reunion, this is a convenience. Right place, right time kind of thing, or whatever grown-ups say. There is nowhere else for me to go, and apparently Frankie, my older brother, has been looking for me.

Two birds, one stone and all that.

Nobody really wants me.

My knees continue to bounce, but this time when Grace looks at me, she's looking at me like she's sad for me, and that makes me want to cry.

"He's not going to like me, is he?" I blurt out.

Her eyes go incredibly wide. "Who said that? Of course he's going to like you. You're his brother."

"Yeah but, my mom and dad are my mom and dad and I don't think they liked me, because they didn't keep me," I rush out in a nervous breath. "Maybe it'll be like that with Frankie."

She frowns and those sad eyes come back.

"I don't think it'll be like that this time." Grace crouches down in front of me, her green eyes staring right at me. "Sometimes meeting new people is hard. But do you know what I do when I'm in a tough situation?"

I shrug. "What?"

She leans forward, as if it's the world's biggest secret. "Sometimes," she starts. "When I'm super scared or super nervous, I close my eyes." She taps her index finger on each of my eyes, forcing me to close them. "I close my eyes and then I count.

"One Mississippi," she whispers. "Two Mississippi. Three Mississippi. Now you do it, and take a deep breath in between each one, okay?"

I stupidly do as she says. Counting and breathing.

It kind of works, but I'm not going to tell her, because I'll probably never use it again.

"Grace." An older lady comes into Grace's office. "Lennox's brother is here."

Grace lets out a loud exhale as she grabs my hands and stands me up. "Are you ready?"

I nod frantically.

"Come on, hold my hand and we'll go and meet him."

She leads me outside her office, and I quickly close my eyes for good measure. It can't hurt.

*One Mississippi. Two Mississippi. Three Mississippi.*

# TWO MISSISSIPPI
## SAMUEL: TEN YEARS OLD

"Do you need me to help you dry your hair?"

"Mom," I whine. "I told you, I can do this on my own now."

With a towel wrapped around my waist, and the blow-dryer in my hand, I wait for my mom to leave the bathroom.

When the door clicks closed, I tip my head upside down—just like I've seen my dad do a hundred times—and let the warm air dry my hair.

*One Mississippi. Two Mississippi. Three Mississippi. Four...*

A hard and loud knock startles me, and I turn off the blow-dryer. The bathroom door opens and my dad walks in. "How are you doing, bud?"

Irritated, I huff. "Why do you and Mom keep coming in? I know how to do my own hair."

Despite my annoyance, he smiles at me and reaches for the blow-dryer. "Can I help you?"

I fold my arms across my chest. "I'm going to be eleven soon, Dad. I can get myself ready."

"I know you can, but maybe I like helping you." He places a hand on my shoulder. "Face the mirror."

Doing as I'm told, I turn and stare at our reflection. Even though I'm only ten years old, there's no mistaking that I look exactly like my dad. He calls me his "mini-me" and I pretend to hate the nickname, but really, if there was ever a person in the world I wanted to be like—with a matching beard and to be the same height—it was him.

And that includes having the same long, curly, blond hair he has. "What number were you up to?" he asks.

"I told Mom I'm big enough to do it on my own," I protest.

"I know." He grabs the blow-dryer and asks again, "What number?"

"Four," I answer.

He runs his fingers through the wet strands of my hair. "Let's start back at one."

He turns on the blow-dryer and starts counting. "One Mississippi. Two Mississippi. Three Mississippi."

My dad loves to count. When he's angry, happy, or sad. He says it gives your brain a few extra seconds to work out what to do next.

When he reaches the number ten I join in and we both count to twenty, the irritation fading and a slow smile that matches my dad's spreads across my face.

"There you go," he states as the noise from the blow-dryer reduces to nothing. "Now you won't sleep with wet hair."

"Can we finish reading that book tonight?" I ask.

"Of course." My dad ruffles my now dry hair. "I'll wait for you in your room."

When he leaves, I quickly put on my underwear and pajamas, then toss my dirty clothes and towel in the clothes hamper. I bump into my mom in the hallway on the way to my bedroom.

"Where's the fire?" she asks, gripping my shoulders and holding me in place.

"Sorry, Mom," I say too quickly. "I need to get to bed so Dad and I can read the last two chapters of my book."

"Slow down or you'll hurt yourself, honey," she says, holding me in place. "He isn't going anywhere."

"I know, I know," I rush out. "Can I go now?"

She kisses the top of my head. "Love you."

"Love you too."

I whiz around her and run to my room. My dad is lying on my bed with his hands around his mouth like a megaphone. "I'm counting to three, Samuel, hurry up and jump in."

*One Mississippi. Two Mississippi. Three Mississippi.*

# THREE MISSISSIPPI
## RHYS: SEVENTEEN YEARS OLD

"Rhys, put your sister down," my mom orders.

"No," I say flatly. "She's crying. Why do you let her cry so much?"

"It's called self-soothing," she says, walking upstairs, like I have half a clue of what the hell that is. "That way she knows how to settle herself sometimes and doesn't always need to be picked up."

"Sounds barbaric if you ask me. Look how quiet she is now." I kiss the top of my sister's head, literally inhaling her brand-new baby smell. I'm completely smitten with her. "I'm not going to let her cry like that if I'm home," I tell my mom. "You can forget about it."

"Suits me fine," she calls out from her bedroom. "You can deal with all the crazy night feeding hours when you're home too."

I don't bother responding because I know she doesn't believe me. Instead, I continue to hold Kayla as I make my way up to her bedroom. We settle in the rocking chair until it lulls us both to sleep.

When I open my eyes, I realize the room is a lot darker and Kayla is no longer in my arms. My heart starts to race as I launch myself out of the rocking chair and straight down the stairs and into the kitchen.

"Where is she?" I breathe out, my head swiveling around the room. "Where is she?"

My father comes out of his den, glass of scotch in hand. "What's gotten up your ass?" he asks.

Distressed, I run my hands through my hair. "Where's Kayla? She was sleeping on my chest."

"You sure she didn't roll off you? Or maybe you squashed her." He chuckles, and I struggle to see just how funny he thinks this is.

"Are you kidding?" I spit out. "How is that helpful? For real, how is you joking about her falling off even the slightest bit funny? Fucking idiot," I mumble.

I wave him off and turn to make my way up the stairs to look for my mom and Kayla. Just as I'm about to climb the first step, a hand grabs the collar of my shirt and yanks me off the stairs. My father pushes me up against the wall, his gross whisky breath fanning my face.

"What did you just call me?" he asks. "Tell me. What did I just hear you say?"

I don't respond, and not because I'm scared of him.

"Tell me," he yells.

I don't take the bait. I don't fight back against the man who seems to have some superiority complex when he drinks.

"Let me go." I push his hands off from around my neck. "I'm going to find Mom."

"You should've hit me," he says, his words coming out a little slurred. "Got yourself a good night's sleep out of it, I'm sure."

I throw my shoulder into him as I move out of his space. I walk up the stairs, leaving him behind, knowing like a dog with a bone, he will always come back.

*One Mississippi. Two Mississippi. Three Mississippi.*

"Oh, I forgot," he calls up after me. "Your mother took Kayla to your aunt's house. I guess they'll be back later on."

# EPILOGUE
## RHYS

EIGHT MONTHS LATER

Samuel nudges my shoulder. "How many times are you going to check that thing?"

I wait as the flight path screen shows up to let us know how long we've been flying for and just how long we've got left before we arrive in Japan.

*Fifteen minutes till landing.*

I would like to say that after my overdose, my father and I went to family counseling, repaired our differences, and now speak to each other regularly. But that not only would be the biggest lie I've ever told, it's also highly unlikely.

Because Joel Denser is a man who could do no wrong; it's everybody else who falls short.

Including me.

*Especially* me.

Six months ago, this revelation would have crippled me. It nearly did. But after a lot of work, I'm coming to realize that not everything between my father and I was about my addiction.

Somewhere along the way I forgot that my father and I never really got along. That somewhere in between Kayla being born and me deciding that I enjoyed the way drugs made me feel, I forgot that our father-son relationship had already become non-existent.

His lack of empathy and unrealistic expectations made sure we would never see eye to eye, and when he realized Kayla and I were joined at the hip, regardless of her disability or our age gap, he became jealous.

And what a revelation that was.

One I wouldn't have ever known about if it wasn't for my mother's moment of good conscience when she visited me in the hospital after my overdose. It was unexpected, and seeing her so bound to him, made me choose empathy over apathy when it came to her.

She pretends the conversation never happened, and that she didn't rat out my dad, and I let her. Because the only thing I want from her is to finally be able to see my sister.

"Ladies and gentlemen, please sit down and fasten your seat belts. Cabin crew, prepare for landing."

*One Mississippi. Two Mississippi. Three Mississippi.*

The announcement makes my heart thump against my chest, and I find myself squeezing Lennox's and Samuel's hands. In sync, both of them lean in and kiss me on the cheek.

They're like a well-oiled machine.

If you'd told me six months ago when I was lying in a hospital bed that this would be my life, I would've laughed in your face. But these two men changed the game for me.

There's been a lot of learning for all three of us. And there's also been a lot of unlearning. It hasn't been easy, but ask me any day of the week if it's been worth it, and the answer's the same.

*Always.*

I didn't think we would make it here, but there were perks to being sober for six months, and that included being financially responsible for myself. It meant my dad didn't control me under the guise of helping me get back on my feet. It meant moving out with my two beautiful boyfriends and starting a life together that is only ours.

It meant learning to live a happy and healthy life. One that increased tenfold the minute I decided to cut him out of my life. When I stopped wanting and needing his approval, I stopped having a point to prove.

And lastly, it meant buying plane tickets with our own money to see Kayla for the first time in six years. To say I'm nervous would be an understatement. Just like my mom promised, we started small. Kayla is very well-versed in technology, so texting and FaceTime are like child's play.

I expected hesitancy and maybe even indifference. I had no idea what she knew of me, or if she even knew me at all. But it appeared like my mother had saved the day one more time.

It was effortless, she had a personality like a firecracker and she loved me more than I deserved.

One day when she's old enough to understand, I'll apologize.

I will apologize for putting her in danger. I will apologize for leaving her alone. But most of all, I will apologize for all the times I didn't try harder to make it right.

I will apologize for the times I let my addiction win, and for all the years we didn't get to have because of it.

But for now, we're in the present.

And my men and I are disembarking the plane at a pace that makes me want to scream.

Lennox's chin lands on my shoulder. "I can't hear, but I can still sense you cursing about this wait." I flip him the bird, and he chuckles. "I know you're nervous, but everything is on schedule and she's going to be waiting for you as soon as we collect our bags."

I know he's trying to reassure me, but it's a fruitless job at this point. I barely made it through the flight and I could no longer be calm or still.

When we finally make it to baggage claim, Samuel grabs a fistful of my shirt and pulls me to him, pressing his mouth to mine.

*One Mississippi. Two Mississippi. Three Mississippi.*

"Breathe for me, okay?" When I avert my gaze and choose not to respond, he inhales loudly and exhales exactly the same. "Do it, baby, please."

Huffing in defeat, I meet his gaze. "Pulled out the 'baby'? Really?"

"I do whatever works, *baby*." He kisses me again and then releases his hold on me. "I'm gonna hang back with the bags, and you just let me know what you need me to do and when."

"You don't have to hang back."

"I don't want to overwhelm her," he says. "If it wasn't for the fact that you might run into your dad, I would've suggested Lennox and I didn't come at all."

It was probably the biggest fight we've all ever had to date. But the make-up sex makes me look back on it a little more fondly than I would've otherwise.

When my sobriety hit the six-month mark, there was no need to question what was next on my to-do list, but when I suggested coming to Japan by myself, neither one of them agreed. In a perfect world, we would all go and it wouldn't be a financial burden on any of us, but that isn't the world we live in.

So, when I said I wanted to come alone, that was my only reason for suggesting it.

I wasn't thinking about the trip itself or the fact that my dad would be around Kayla and possibly attempt to torment me.

Their need to want to come for this reason, made me think that they didn't trust me in his presence, that they didn't trust my sobriety and because of that I couldn't be alone.

That thought hurt.

It was warranted, but it still hurt.

Because while I understood it, we were in such a good place. *I* was in such a good place. There was therapy and meetings and work. I had just started classes to become an accredited sign language teacher, and I hadn't felt like I was living a life that was mine like this in such a long time.

But then we had the talk and they explained that their fears and distrust had nothing to do with me and everything to do with my father, and all the puzzle pieces fit a little better.

They loathed him. We didn't talk about him often, but when he did come up in conversation, the anger they felt for him was unrivaled. In all honesty, it made me love them so much more. And even though I don't think he'll bother with us while we're here, there is a part of me that is glad I will never have to face him alone.

Eventually, Samuel locates our bags, and stacks them carefully on the trolley. The three of us manage to hold hands as we leave the terminal and wait for my family to meet us.

Naturally, I spot her first, and my hands tighten in theirs. I watch my mother navigate Kayla through the crowd of travelers. She's so grown up, it almost makes me want to double over in pain at how beautiful she is and how much time with her I've missed.

But I do my very best to not think like that anymore. I can't agonize over the past because I can't change it, but I sure can put the same amount of energy into living in the here and now.

As soon as the pathway to me is clear, Kayla lets go of my mother's hand and runs to me.

She runs to me.

She runs to *me.*

Opening my arms, she jumps straight into them and I fold her into me. Tears spill over almost immediately as my heart swells, feeling well and truly whole for the first time in six years.

I lean back a little bit to give her room to communicate if she needs it. She glances between Lennox and Samuel, both of whom she has met over FaceTime numerous times, and surprises us all when she throws her dainty but long arms around Lennox's waist and then scoots over to do the same to Samuel.

She is just as excited to be a part of my life as I am to be in hers. When we reach the town car my mother provided, I help Kayla into the back seat and wait to be alone with my men.

"Wait," I say before they climb in.

Reaching for their hands, I bring them both to my lips, kissing them incessantly. I hold up a finger for both of them to wait and then I pull out my cell phone.

We don't use it as often as we once had, now that after almost ten months of learning and persistence, Lennox knows everything I do.

But every now and then, I go back to the day I was released from the hospital. The day that reminds me of the beauty of life and all I would miss if I weren't here. The day that the three of us started a new little tradition.

I unlock my phone and hand it to Lennox, then sign the word "read" with my two hands.

He follows my instructions, and I watch his throat bob as he finds exactly what I left there for him.

Lennox clears his throat before glancing at the both of us.

"I love you," he says, reading off the screen. "I love you both. I love you individually. I love us all together. All my todays are for you, and all my tomorrows are because of you."

"You're killing me here," he says, his voice cracking.

I chuckle softly as he continues.

"I'll love you when it's desperate and dire. I'll love you when it's beautiful and boring. I'll love you from this breath to the next, and for every breath after."

Lennox lifts his tear-filled eyes to meet ours, and the three of us raise our hands and sign it at the same time.

The first sign I taught them.

The only sign that matters.

*I love you.*

———

**Pre-order Clem + Zara's Sapphic Romance**

**Did you enjoy Unloved?**

If you want to see more of Lennox, Rhys and Samuel, click the following link to receive a bonus epilogue in the New Year.

**Newsletter Sign Up**

———

**Want to know more about Arlo and Frankie?**
**Find out what happens in Unwanted, the first book in The Unlucky Ones Series: A second chance, gay romance**

———

**Want more LGBTQIA+ Romance from Marley Valentine?**

**Without You**
**Devilry: A Teacher/Student Romance**
**Unforgettable (Vino & Veritas)**
**What We Broke**
**Unlikely (The Unlucky Ones)**

**Tragedy brought us together, but something stronger made me want to stay.**

Julian was the boy next door. My brother's best friend, he fit with my family in ways I never could. While he and Rhett went on to play house, I left the only life I knew, desperate for a fresh start.

Until everything changed.

Heartache came along, and the aftermath of my brother's death was here to stay. I was now face to face with Julian more than I ever wanted to be.

Being around him brought up all my insecurities, forced me to deal with hard truths, and conjured up feelings I had no business entertaining. He wasn't the man I thought I knew. He was complex and layered, and inherently beautiful in all the ways I'd never noticed.

Not on another person.

Not on another man.

Not until him.

**PURCHASE WITHOUT YOU: A BROTHER'S BEST FRIEND ROMANCE**

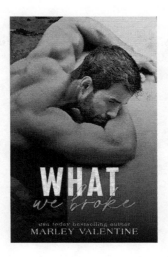

**From USA Today Bestselling Author, Marley Valentine comes a brand new, marriage in crisis, hurt/comfort, standalone, gay romance.**

**If someone asked me to describe our love story, I would only need to use two words.**

**Before and After.**

When I met Leonardo Ricci, he was determined I would only be a fling, while I was certain he was my forever.

Seven years later, we're the perfect couple. Happy, married, and in love–in sickness and health, till death do us part.
At least until the unthinkable happens.

Now we can't look at each other. We don't sleep in the same bed. We can't even be in the same room. The loss is too great and the pain runs too deep.

But this man is the love of my life. I convinced him once, and I would be damned if I couldn't do it again. I would be damned if I couldn't fix what we broke.

**PURCHASE WHAT WE BROKE: A MARRIAGE-IN-CRISIS ROMANCE**

**I couldn't tell you when I fell in love with Gael Herrera, but I wish I knew how to make it stop.**

Falling in love with a straight man is a rookie mistake. But falling in love with my soon-to-be-married-to-a-woman best friend is nothing but heartache.

Through all the years, and all the men I've fooled around with, he's always been at the back of my mind. An unrequited crush I wish I could shake. A dream that was never going to come true.

When I whisk him off to a surprise bachelor party weekend in Vegas, I surrender to the idea that this is an opportunity for me to finally let go of my feelings for him and say goodbye.

But after a heated exchange and an even hotter kiss, everything I thought I knew about our friendship changed.

Maybe I had it wrong. Maybe, after all this time, we were more than best friends. Maybe, just maybe, he felt it too.

**PURCHASE ACHE: A FRIENDS TO LOVERS ROMANCE**

Two halves of a whole, Arlo Bishop and I were both unwanted kids brought together by the foster system. Dealing with the aftermath of neglect and abandonment, we grew up side by side and found solace in one another.

We wanted.

We needed.

We loved.

Desperately.

But somewhere along the way, Arlo wanted and needed and loved drugs more. So, I did the only thing I could and broke my own heart to save his.

Now, four years later, I'm back in L.A. and face-to-face with my past. Not only does the pain and hurt of our mistakes linger between us, but so do our feelings.

I didn't plan on a second chance, fear of history repeating itself making it hard to forgive and even harder to forget. But with only one touch, one kiss, I was taken back to where it all started.

Two halves of a whole, Arlo Bishop and I were made for for each other. But we were no longer the unwanted foster kids.

We were grown men.

And I wanted nothing more than him.

**PURCHASE UNWANTED: A SECOND CHANCE ROMANCE**

**Attending King University was at the top of my bucket list. Falling in love with my professor wasn't.**

Earning a full scholarship to King University was my hard earned ticket out of hell. I'm happy to be away from the small town I grew up in and all the equally small minded people who live there.

King was going to be my safe haven. A place where I could leave the old me behind and finally grow into the young man my family had desperately tried to hide away.

Diving head first into new experiences, new friends, and parties, I didn't expect to run straight into the one thing I wasn't ready for.

His arms are welcoming, his body is addictive and his lips are heaven. Cole Huxley is everything I could fall in love with, except for one problem... I never wanted to fall for my professor.

**PURCHASE DEVILRY: A TEACHER/STUDENT ROMANCE**

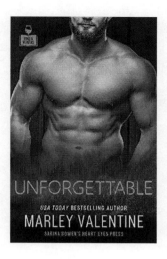

One night with Reeve Hale wasn't enough. I knew it when I kissed him, I knew it when I slept with him, and I was certain of it when I walked out of his motel room the very next day.

So when the shy, gorgeous man is introduced as our newest employee at Vino and Veritas, I can't help but conjure up all the ridiculous ways to convince him to repeat that unforgettable night. Like asking him to be my fake boyfriend at my sister's upcoming wedding.
Only, I didn't expect him to say yes.

Playing pretend shouldn't feel this real. Especially when Reeve is planning on leaving Vermont after the summer.

We agreed to one night. We negotiated a fake relationship. But I'm the one who broke our terms. I wasn't supposed to fall in love and he was never supposed to be so unforgettable.

**<u>PURCHASE UNFORGETTABLE: A WORK PLACE/ FAKE RELATIONSHIP ROMANCE</u>**

# ACKNOWLEDGMENTS

If you made it here, you made it to the end of the book and I hope you truly enjoyed it.

All my books are a labour of love, but this one put me through the wringer from the get go. I want to say a wish I knew why, but I only know that this story refused to be rushed, it refused to be the story I plotted and it refused to come out on time.
If you love it, thank you. If you don't then hey, I have a few other books you can choose from.

Firstly I want to thank everyone who is always in my corner. You make the impossible days a little less so and I don't think you know how much that means to me.

Kacey, Laura, Jodi and Jill, thank you for always talking me off the ledge.

Shauna, thank you as usual for being there when the world shits itself all over my timelines.

Becca at The Author Agency, thank you so much for putting up with me. But also for making this release go as smooth as it possibly could.

Judy, Chele and Roger, thank you so much for all your advice and feedback as I wrote this book. I'm so grateful to the extra eyes on it.

My mum and my sister: no words will ever be enough to say thank you for helping me make my dreams come true.

To my Andrew and the boys: I love you. x

Until next time. Much Peace and Love.And that's it from me.
Until next time.
Much Peace and Love.

# ABOUT THE AUTHOR

*Marley Valentine*

Living in Sydney, Australia with her family, Marley Valentine is a USA Today bestselling author and a former social worker who uses her past experiences to write real life, emotional and heartfelt contemporary romance.

She enjoys mixing it up with all types of romance pairings, incorporating all forms of life, lust and love as her characters embark on their journey to their happily ever after.

When she's not busy writing her own stories, she spends most of her time immersed in the words of her favourite authors.

Marley enjoys interacting with her readers so please feel free to reach out to her via Facebook, Instagram, email and/or subscribe to her newsletter.

*Other Books by Marley Valentine*

**Reclaim | Revive | Rectify**

*MM Romance Books*

**Devilry | Without You | Ache|Unforgettable | What We Broke**

*The Unlucky Ones*

Unwanted | Unloved | Unlikely

*Find Marley*

Facebook | Facebook Reader Group | Amazon Author
Page | Goodreads Author
Page | Twitter | Instagram | Website | BookBub | Newsletter

Made in the USA
Monee, IL
09 October 2024

477f103b-61dd-4dc6-b236-04526fe6c3a7R01